Forever My

Princess

TAMARA

Gill

COPYRIGHT

Forever My Princess
The Royal House of Atharia, Book 3
Copyright © 2021 by Tamara Gill
Cover Art by Wicked Smart Designs
& Chris Cocozza Illustration
Editor Grace Bradley Editing
All rights reserved.

ISBN: 978-0-6453216-0-9

CHAPTER 1

*P*rincess Elena of Atharia sat in the opulent wingback chair in her sister's new London home and waited for her friend Lady Margaret Villiers to arrive.

She had sent word almost two hours ago for her to call, and yet still, she had not arrived. Elena stood, pacing back and forth between her chair and the mantel, the clock clicking down the time with an annoying tick.

What could have kept her? Margaret had not sent word that she could not attend her summons.

Elena frowned. For her plan to work, she needed Margaret's loyalty and silence for the next month at least. The many letters she had written to her sister crinkled in her pocket, and she patted her leg, ensuring herself they were still there.

She had spent hours penning them, wanting to ensure her sister Alessa never assumed she was not where she was supposed to be. That she would not come looking for her for the next month at least.

A footman knocked and came into the room, bowing.

"Your Highness, Lady Margaret Villiers wishes an audience."

Elena whirled about, seeing her friend grinning behind the footman's back. "Thank you, John. We will have tea if you please," she commanded the footman, watching as Margaret came into the room and closed the door behind her.

Elena met her across the room, taking her friend's hands. "Oh, I'm so very pleased you are here. I did not think you would attend, and then I was not sure what I would do."

Margaret, sensing the worry in Elena's tone, frowned. "Whatever is the matter that you are all aflutter? I thought you would be busy packing for Kew Palace? What fun we shall have for the next month. Do you think King George will attend after all?"

Elena gestured toward a chair. "We need to talk. Please sit, Margaret," she asked her friend, joining her on the settee.

"What is it that you need to discuss so urgently?" Margaret asked, trepidation in her tone. "Are you about to tell me you're not going to attend the house party? I shall be ever so disappointed if you do not."

Guilt pricked her conscience that her friend's concern was about to come to fruition. But there was no way around it. She needed to leave London to remove herself from the endless cycle of balls and parties. Having entered society last year in Atharia, Elena felt she had done nothing but parade herself before eligible young men who were looking for a bride.

She no longer wanted to play such games. A month away at a country house with an elderly lady who needed her, a woman who had once been her mother's closest friend, was just what she needed. If only to regain her composure, to prepare herself for a union that would eventually come.

She was not fool enough not to know that she would eventually marry a man whom her sisters deemed appropriate. But it was not how she wanted to choose a spouse. She wanted to fall in love, to marry her best friend. The gentlemen in town were all so charming and complimentary, so much so that their constant flattery made her teeth ache they were so sweet.

And false, she accepted. None of them would love her for the woman she was inside her royal shell. They loved the power and influence that came with marrying her, what she brought to the union monetarily and in status only. She could not marry such a man. Being gone from London may help her rally to stand firm and not settle for anything but the best.

"I'm afraid I'm going to disappoint you, Margaret dear, but I do hope you'll support me as your dearest friend, for I shall need your help, even if I'm not with you at Kew Palace."

"What do you need me to do? Or better yet," Margaret added, raising one questionable brow, "what is it that you're going to do?"

"As to that," Elena said, nerves and expectation making her stomach flip. She had never been adventurous. After being left at the castle in Atharia when her sister Alessa had escaped, she had done all she could to become invisible.

Such a temperament and desire had not left her since coming out and being in society. She was no longer so comfortable in boisterous and crowded ballrooms. She would much prefer a country ride or a long walk in beautiful gardens to a ball. And she could not stomach false-hoods, and there were many directed at her from the men who wished to make her their wife.

"I have taken a position as a lady's companion to the Dowager Marchioness of Lyon in Somerset. She was friends with my mama during her coming out, but we have never met. I know she will not recognize me. I will be working for her ladyship under the alias of Miss Elena Smith. I leave for the estate tomorrow, the same day I'm supposed to leave for the house party at Kew Palace."

Margaret's mouth gaped, and Elena hoped she had not bitten off too much for her friend to take in or for her to do. "Tell me you're willing to help me. I truly do not wish to attend the house party. I need some time away from London and the madness that my title brings into my life. A month in the county will be the perfect escape, and I shall return in four weeks, ready to find a husband and marry."

"Really?" Margaret scoffed, chuckling a little at her words. "But what of Lord Lyon? Will he not be home? From what I know of him, he never attends the Season, something about a rift that happened years ago with his father and King George, I believe, here in London."

"That does not mean he does not need a companion for his mother, but from what the correspondence has stated so far, forwarded to me from the servant registry office I've been hired through, he is to return to town."

"Well," Margaret said with a surprised exhalation. "I did not think he would ever come to London. He is one of those country gentlemen who never comes to town, but I'm sure his return here will cause a lot of hearts to flutter."

Elena did not care how many hearts fluttered in London for the marquess, so long as she had a lovely, relaxing four weeks looking after his mother and keeping her company. A month of long country walks, of reading and sitting before the hearth, not having to attend a ball or soiree, or a royal event would be a pleasure indeed.

"Perhaps he intends to find a wife, like so many other gentlemen of our acquaintance. Nevertheless, his plans are not my concern. I have been hired as Miss Smith and Miss Smith I shall be for the next four weeks."

Margaret pinned her with a disapproving stare. "And may I ask how it is, *Princess Elena*," she said, accentuating her title, "that you will get away with such a plan? Your sister is in London and will want to know that you are safe and well, especially after her own safety scare last Season. I do not see how you can get away with this foolery at all."

Elena had it all planned and this plan was the reason she had asked Margaret to call today, for she too featured in her escape. She reached into her pocket and pulled out the six letters she had written to Alessa. "You know that I adore you as a friend, and I do need your help if I'm to succeed. Will you help me?"

Margaret's mouth opened and closed several times, her eyes wide with surprise. "Me?" she said, pointing to herself. "What is it that I'm supposed to do? Need I remind you that you have a sister who is a queen and another who is a very independent, strong-willed princess right here in town? Should either of them find out I helped you escape, I shall be strung up and hung from the nearest gallows."

Elena chuckled. "I can always count on you to make me laugh, but you are wrong. Neither sister will ever find out. If you can have these letters sent over the next four weeks while you're at Kew Palace, Alessa will be none the wiser. She will not know that I'm, in fact, in Somerset."

"And if your sister calls in at Kew Palace. The estate is not so very far away from London."

Elena waved her friend's concerns away. "She is far too busy with her charities to be worried about me at a house party for a month. While I have little doubt that she will lecture me to behave and remember my manners before I go, she will never think that I shall not attend at all."

"And what of King George who sent out all these invitations? Will he not out you to your siblings should he find out you did not attend?"

"No," Elena stated, shaking her head and not the least concerned with that part of her plan either. "King George will not attend, even if he has invited us all to his country estate. You know he prefers to keep his select few and himself locked away at Windsor."

"Even so, I feel nervous about deceiving your sisters. They will be ever so cross with me should they find out."

Elena reached out and took Margaret's hand. "Listen, they will not be angry with you; they will be angry with me." She reached back into her pocket and pulled out another letter. "This is all the information of where I am and the dates I shall be away. Lord Lyon was very particular as to the time that he required a companion for his mama, and it was perfect luck that they coincided with the house party at Kew. Do not worry at all. You enjoy your time away from town, hand these letters to a footman at the palace, and that is all you need to concern yourself with."

While Margaret considered her decision, Elena wondered if she had been foolish in thinking she could do such a thing. To run away, even if only for four weeks, was still a risk. Her heart went out to her friend, worrying so. "If you do not wish to, that is perfectly well too, Margaret.

I would never ask you to do anything that you're uncomfortable or disagree with. I can change my plans and come to the house party, and no one would ever be the wiser to what I wanted to do."

Margaret bit her bottom lip in thought. "No, I shall help you. You are my closest friend, and you deserve to do what you think will make you ready for marriage. An institution that we all shall have to face very soon, I should imagine. I want to help you, and I shall post your letters. But," Margaret said, stemming Elena's attempt to pull her into a hug, "should your sisters arrive and inquire of your whereabouts or want to see you, I will tell them the truth. Are you in agreement?" she asked her, holding up her hand and sticking out her smallest finger.

"What are you doing with your hand?" Elena asked, having never seen anyone hold out their finger in such a way.

"This is a pinkie promise. Should you shake my finger with your own smallest finger, it will mean that you agree to my terms, and you are free to travel to Somerset and Lord Lyon's estate."

Elena stared at Margaret's smallest digit, thinking over her friend's terms, which were utterly appropriate and fair. She hooked her finger around Margaret's. "I swear and agree to what you say, and I thank you so very much."

Hope and excitement thrummed through her veins over her forthcoming month away from town, from people and noise, scandal and negotiation. How wonderful her time in Somerset would be, and tomorrow morning when the carriage arrived to take her away, she would be ready and willing to transform into Miss Elena Smith, Princess Elena no more.

CHAPTER 2

Theodore Ward, the Marquess of Lyon stared out over his land and breathed deep the crisp morning air. The land, with its rolling green hills, the forests filled with deer and game, the few fields he had left plowed and planted by his family for five centuries filled him with a mix of pride and despair.

Lyon Estate was his home, where he envisioned raising his children and bringing home his bride. Under no circumstances would he allow the greedy royal family of England to win the war they pledged against his father and following heirs.

He kicked his mount, cantering down the hill and returning home. One of the largest in England, the residence housed over a hundred rooms, some he doubted he had seen. All of them in need of refurbishment or repair of some sort, and none of the renovations being completed due to his lack of funds.

But not for long. The next day, he was to London once the lady's companion he hired to care for his mother arrived.

He hoped the woman he sourced from the servant registry service in London did not send him a lady of inadequate abilities. He needed a woman with a kind heart and a gentle hand. His mother deserved nothing less.

His horse attempted a jump over a small bush, and a smile quirked Theo's lips. He would miss his morning rides, overlooking his land, what was left of it at least, and seeing his home, as disheveled as it was, glistening in the morning sun.

A carriage rolled through the gates, and he could only assume it was the lady's companion from London. She had said in her correspondence she would be staying the night at the local village not far from his estate and arriving on time as agreed.

Her letters were very well-written with a capable hand, and he had high hopes she would do the job very well for the short amount of time he needed her.

He walked up the drive, watching as the carriage rolled to a halt before the double front doors of his estate. A man seated beside the driver jumped down, lowering the steps and opening the carriage door.

Curiosity got the better of Theo, and he kicked his mount into a canter, wanting to meet his new servant and take stock if she would do well enough.

He pulled his mount to a halt and jumped down, his attention snapping to the delicate, kid-leather gloved hand reaching out to take the footman's assistance.

His mama, as much as he loved her, could be a little snobbish and curt when a censored glare was not curtailing her tongue.

About to step forward, Theo's legs became logs of wood at the vision of the woman stepping onto his grav-

9

eled drive. She looked up at the estate, pleasure crossing her features as she took in his ancestral home.

But that was not what had his body as still as death. For if he were indeed passed from this earth, it was surely because he had viewed an angel.

He snapped his mouth shut and took a fortifying breath. The woman was to be his mother's companion, and while he could admire her beauty, that was where it would end.

But by jove, she was more than beautiful. She was stunning, enough to render him speechless. Her skin was like alabaster, her hair as dark as night, and her body, even under the heavy traveling cloak, was one made for sin.

If only he could have such a woman for himself.

He shook the thought aside. She was a lady's companion for a reason, and that reason was certainly not because she was an heiress who could save him and his estate from financial ruin.

His wife had to be rich, so very rich that no money lenders, no banks, or even The Crown could ever come knocking on his doors ever again.

"Miss Elena Smith, I presume," he said, finding his voice and bowing before her.

She turned, surprise written across her features at having not seen him before she laughed, a tinkling sound that was indeed as heavenly as he imagined it would be.

Everything about this woman seemed divine. If it were not for her hair that put paid to her angelic background, he would be certain she was indeed from the heavens.

She came over to him, giving him her gloved fingers. "Indeed it is. Lord Lyon, I presume," she said, dipping into a curtsy.

He smiled, reminding himself that his duty toward this

woman went further than admiring her person all day long. He gestured toward the front doors. "Allow me to escort you inside. We shall discuss your employment in my library before I introduce you to the Dowager Marchioness of Lyon, Lady Lyon."

"Of course," she agreed, stepping forward and heading toward the doors. Theo followed her before leading the way into the library. He ignored the pinch of embarrassment that marked his skin at the aged and worn upholstery and furniture, walls that needed new wallpapers, and windows that required a thorough clean. His staff were few, and there were simply too many other jobs falling onto the shoulders of too few. Dirty windows were the least of his concerns.

He picked up a chair that sat against the wall and placed it before his desk, gesturing for Miss Smith to take a seat. She did as he bade, and he sank into his own chair, four feet of mahogany the only thing separating them.

"You found the estate alright then, Miss Smith? Some have difficulty finding the turn into the grounds," he mentioned, making small talk and trying to put Miss Smith at ease. Although from taking in her countenance, she did not seem at all nervous to be before a lord or taking on the responsibilities of a dowager marchioness.

"The coachman was familiar with the location of Lyon Estate as he lives in the village nearby. It was no trouble at all finding your home, which I must compliment you on. It is lovely indeed."

Theo found himself smiling at her words. As pretty as they were, he knew them to be a lie. His estate was showing the signs of neglect, of poor cash flow, which he would soon remedy.

The would-be ladies in London this year were in need

11

of a titled husband as much as he needed their inheritances. The deal was a good one for all involved.

"I must mention, Miss Smith that the Dowager Marchioness of Lyon, my mother, is ill of health. She has aged in the few years since my father's passing, and I fear that it will not be long that I shall have her with me. I would like the assurance that the month that I require you to be here, that you are kind and attentive to her, allow her any little vices she desires and keep her safe. I was assured you came highly recommended by the agency to meet all my requirements. Are you still in agreement to do as I ask?" Theo held his breath, needing her to agree so he could make final preparations to remove himself to town. Having heard all of her duties, if Miss Smith now wished to leave, he did not know what he would do.

She nodded, smiling, and he felt the breath in his lungs expel on a sigh. Her beauty was certainly something to get used to. He did not think he'd ever seen anyone as perfect as the woman before him. There was something about her, a poise, a regalness that spoke of good breeding and aristocratic blood.

He dismissed the thought. She was a servant, a lady's companion, and while she may have come from money once, she certainly had no link to it now if this was the position she had to take up.

"Of course. I'm prepared to look after the marchioness and keep her safe and happy these next four weeks. In fact, I'm looking forward to all the entertainment we shall do. I hope you do not mind, but I have thought up some of my own ways to keep her occupied if you would give me leave to use them."

Miss Smith was like a breath of fresh air into his musty, old house. As much as he loved the estate, the old girl needed repairs and a lot of blunt spent. With the knowledge of Miss Smith here with his mama, he could remove himself to town, knowing he had not put his parent in jeopardy.

"Of course, you may do whatever you wish if she agrees. She cannot swim, however, Miss Smith, so perhaps do not attempt to swim in the lake while I'm not here."

She chuckled, her brown eyes, or perhaps hazel, bright with amusement. "I shall not, I promise," she agreed. "Is the dowager marchioness about, my lord? I should like to meet her if you're happy with me starting my employment here in earnest."

Theo stood. "Come, we shall go meet her now. She is in the upstairs drawing room. She uses that room above any else in the house as it gets both morning and afternoon sun being on the west wing."

"How lovely." Miss Smith followed him out of the room, and Theo ignored the fact that she would see other parts of the house that needed repair. She would understand soon enough after living here some days that he was a lord after a rich wife, and that is why he left for London.

There was no shame in that fact, even though it irked his soul that his father had died a broken, lost man after the king cheated at the game of cards, fleecing him of land and money he did not deserve to win.

The bastard royal pig that he was.

They made the first-floor landing, and Theo led Miss Smith toward the drawing room, one of the largest rooms in the house. The door was ajar, and he could hear his mother speaking to a maid about stoking the fire with more wood. Why, he could not understand, since England was experiencing a heatwave.

He entered and waited for Miss Smith to stand beside

him. "Mama, may I introduce you to Miss Elena Smith? She's to be your lady's companion for the next month."

His mother lifted her spectacles from her lap, peering through them to take in Miss Smith. Her mouth puckered into a displeased line, and Theo hoped she was not going to be curt or rude to the woman at his side. Certainly, he hoped they would get along well so he could leave without any concerns.

"Hmm, so you're the miss to coddle me like a babe." His mother dismissed Miss Smith with a disgruntled sniff. "I do not take well to being treated like a baby, so do not attempt to do whatever it was that my son has suggested to you. I'm a marchioness, not a moron. I still have my wits about me, so do not attempt to make me into a pet who requires saving. I will not abide it."

Miss Smith glanced up at Theo, but he was mistaken if he thought to see fear and regret. Instead, he saw resilience and determination, and his interest in the peculiar Miss Smith was piqued.

Who was this young woman?

She moved toward his mama and dipped into a curtsy. "Lady Lyon, it is an honor to meet you, and I'm so glad to have this opportunity to spend the month with you." Miss Smith moved past his mama and sat in a chair at her side. "If you will allow me to speak, I would like to say that I do not want to be your nursemaid any more than you wish to have one. I'm here to keep you company and do whatever you want me to. That is all, nothing more and nothing less."

His mama's brows rose in surprise, and he could see his parent trying to figure out if Miss Smith was trying to play a trick of some kind. Theo bit back a smile, having trouble himself figuring out the young woman.

Mayhap his luck was changing, and his trip to London would be successful. That he would return to Somerset married to a disgustingly wealthy heiress and a parent who was no longer so very annoyed at everyone she came across.

His mother's cane came down hard on the floor, a loud clank making him cringe. "I do not know what game you're playing, Miss Smith. But you are to speak when spoken to and that I'm afraid will not often be. Now do shut up."

Theo groaned. Well, at least he may get one of his wishes true, that of a wealthy bride. His mother, unfortunately, looked well set to remain the termagant she had become in her old age.

CHAPTER 3

*E*lena had tried and failed miserably not to laugh at the dowager's command that she shut up. Never in her life had she ever been spoken to in such a high-handed, commanding way, and as much as it amused her, she also could not help but wonder why her ladyship was so very angry.

Was she angry with her son, perhaps that he was leaving for London and leaving her behind? Maybe she too wanted to go to town and enjoy the Season.

Certainly, there were ladies her ladyship's age who still attended balls and parties, some even commencing illicit love affairs due to their widowed status.

Lord Lyon's visage visibly paled, and he came over beside his mother. "Mother, apologize to Miss Smith. She's here to keep you company while I'm away and nothing more."

"Pfft," her ladyship spat. "I do not need taking care of, but since you insist, I suppose I have no choice." Her ladyship leaned down, picking up a bag of knitting that Elena had not seen, and commenced pulling out her needles.

Elena sat back in the settee, perfectly content to allow her ladyship her time to do what she wanted. She was more than satisfied to be sitting in this drawing room than one in London where she was a special feature for people's entertainments. A princess to ogle and admire.

She clenched her teeth, having had enough of being the perfect royal in town. This month here in Somerset was just what she needed.

A break from all that noise.

Her ladyship flicked her hand at her son, who remained nearby, his unease at leaving Elena with his parent obvious. "You may go, Theodore. I shall not injure Miss Smith," her ladyship stated, not bothering to meet her son's eye.

Lord Lyon sighed. "I do apologize, Miss Smith. Please let me know if my mother does not become more agreeable."

She nodded, having no intention of doing such a thing.

His lordship bowed and left, and Elena wondered if her ladyship would not speak to her and keep silent and occupied with her knitting. Elena watched as her fingers worked fast with the needles and wool. She wished she were as proficient with the task. She struggled to sew, one of the occupations that a lady should excel at never an ability she held.

She could draw, ride a horse, swim, and run well enough, and she was happy to have those abilities instead.

Her ladyship laid down her knitting and pinned her with a disapproving glare. "Now, Miss Smith, if that is what you're calling yourself, you may explain to me what you are about."

Elena felt her mouth gape, and she snapped it closed, unable to comprehend what her ladyship meant and not wanting to find out particularly. She thought back over her trip to Somerset and knew she had not been recognized anywhere. Her ladyship's words made no sense at all.

"I beg your pardon, my lady. I do not know what you mean," she ventured, swallowing the bile that rose in her throat that she'd been found out. Surely not! Lady Lyon had never met her before in her life. She was a stranger to the woman. There was no way she could know she was royalty.

"The moment I saw you, I knew who you were. Your mama and I debuted together. We were friends, you see, and you, my dear, are the spitting image of her. It was like seeing a ghost."

Elena slumped. Her ruse had lasted all of one hour from her arrival to now. She would be required to go to Kew Palace and pretend to enjoy herself. How dreadfully boring and mundane.

Why had she not thought of the possibility that the dowager would have recognized her? It was no secret in the family that she resembled her mother, most of all the daughters of the king and queen. With the dowager a good friend of her mama during their first Season in society, she should have known such an outcome as this could occur.

Damn it all to hell, she inwardly cursed. "I did not think that anyone would remember my mama. She left England so many years ago and has been gone since I was a child." Elena's smile wobbled. "You remember her?"

Lady Lyon reached out, taking her hand and giving it a comforting squeeze. "Oh yes, I remember her well. She was my friend, and you are uncannily similar." She paused. "I had seen your sisters when I was in town last. But I had never laid eyes on you, but the moment you entered the room, I knew you were up to a ruse." Her ladyship raised one brow. "Miss Smith? Surely you could have come up with a less ordinary name than Smith of all that are available."

Elena snorted, supposing her ladyship had a point. "It was the first name that came to mind at the agency when they asked for my surname. I had to think quick, and that was what I came up with."

Her ladyship chuckled. "Well, even so, you're here now, so you had better tell me what all this is about. Why are you here pretending to be a servant, for heaven's sake?"

"Well, as to that…"

"And," her ladyship said, halting her explanation. "There will be no more curtsying to me. You outrank me tenfold. How absurd, a princess curtsying to a marchioness. I have never heard of such a thing."

Elena nodded, but that was the least of her concerns. Now she had to convince her ladyship to let her stay and to not say a word. "I no longer wanted to be in London. I was expected at a country house party at Kew Palace, but I knew even then I would be put up on a pedestal to be admired, to be crowed about that they had met the youngest princess from Atharia. I feel invisible in London. Like I do not have a voice or at least one that anyone wishes to hear. Not me, the real me inside," she said, pointing to her chest. "I wanted to escape, and I read in the paper the advertisement that Lord Lyon was seeking a companion, and so I applied through the servant registry office."

"And your sisters, do they know where you are?"

She pursed her lips, hoping her ladyship would not be mad at her next words. "No, they do not. They believe me to be at Kew, but I have a friend there who is posting letters from me to them, so they will think I'm safe and sound, doing the pretty by attending the party as asked."

"There would be many who would cut off a finger to attend a house party hosted by the King of England."

"Oh, King George will not be in attendance. I can only assume because he finds such outings as boring and ineffective as I do."

Lady Lyon bit back a grin. "You have a forked tongue, my dear, but I suppose being a princess does allow one such freedom." She paused, studying her a moment. "You cannot stay here. You do know that, do you not?"

"But I can," she pressed, clasping her ladyship's hands. "Lord Lyon will be in London from tomorrow, and then it will only be us to keep each other company. And even if his lordship remained, you're a perfectly acceptable chaperone. I do not need anything more."

"I'm sure at times society and my son believe me to be ailing. They will not like that a princess is under the Lyon roof without an adequate chaperone."

"Well," Elena stated, determined to get her way. She wanted to stay at the estate even more now that she knew her ladyship remembered her mama, and knew who she was. "They will never know if you do not tell anyone that I'm here," she hedged. "Nor do I see anyone in my presence who is ailing or infirm. You seem quite sprightly, in my opinion."

"And on top of being a princess, you're now a doctor. Is that correct?"

Elena shrugged, grinning. "If you like, I can be both, but I'd prefer to be your friend and here incognito until I have to return to town in four weeks."

The dowager seemed unmoved, and so there was really only one thing left for Elena to do. "Would you please let me stay? I will not be any trouble, and I shall help as I promised his lordship with assisting you."

Her ladyship scoffed as if she had never heard such a preposterous idea. "You will not. A princess will not fetch for me day and night. I would not think of it."

"As you stated before, I outrank you, so, therefore, it is my choice, is it not?"

Her ladyship's mouth puckered into a disapproving frown, but she did not counter what Elena had stated.

She nodded, pleased that her ladyship understood. Not that she wanted to be high-handed, but she was desperate to remove herself from London. Not forever, but certainly for the few weeks her ruse would allow her to keep away, to hide and refresh her sensibilities to face what was to come. A marriage, family, the possibility that she would stay in England with her new husband and not return to Atharia after her wedding. "Exactly, so it is my choice, and I have stated what I wish to do. Now, shall we play a game of whist or vingt-et-un?"

"Whist if you please," her ladyship conceded, putting down her knitting.

Elena smiled to herself, going to the mantel and ringing for a maid. "I shall have the gaming table set up for us. Would you like tea and biscuits brought in, my lady?"

The notion of a hot repast seemed to please her ladyship more than the thought of Elena staying under her roof without anyone's knowledge. "Yes, thank you, that would be lovely."

Just as her four weeks in Somerset would be perfectly lovely as well.

CHAPTER 4

*L*ater that evening, Lady Lyon sat in her bed, her lady's maid seated on a chair at her side, reading to her from a book she was no longer listening to. "We must do something about my son. He cannot leave the estate now and travel to London. We have to halt his departure, not just tomorrow, but for the remainder of the month."

"We do?" Fanny asked, a confused frown on her brow. "But he's to travel to London to marry, you said. How can he find a wife if he remains in Somerset?"

"Well, while you do not need to concern yourself as to why I want him to remain in Somerset, I do need you to concern yourself with gaining the help of Thomas out in the stable. I know you're both sweet on each other, and he'll do your bidding, and if not yours, then he will certainly do mine."

She contemplated all the ways one would keep a person from departing. Nothing too obvious that her clever son would figure out too soon. But he had to stay. No matter what she had said to Princess Elena earlier that day about her needing to leave, there was no reason why she could not stay while she was in attendance. A dowager was as good a chaperone as anyone. But her son required a rich wife, and there was none richer than a princess from Atharia. With two already off the marriage mart, Elena was all who was left, and she was too charming for words. Intelligent too, her ladyship guessed, and utterly beautiful. Too beautiful to pretend to be a lady's companion, but if that is what she wanted to do, that is what she would allow her to be for the next few weeks at least.

But to keep her son behind these doors had to occur too for her plan to work.

"What would you like me to ask Thomas? I know he's in the stables now, my lady," Fanny said, intrigue burning in her blue gaze.

"Have something go wrong with the carriage. Have Thomas loosen a sprig or bolt or some such without anyone noticing. Enough that the carriage will not be able to be used. My son will not ride all the way to London. Our horses are carriage horses only, and the one mount he has is too old to make it to town."

"Of course, my lady. I shall go to Thomas directly." Fanny stood, placing the chair she had been seated upon beside the wall. "What about the remainder of the days?"

The dowager pursed her lips. "Make sure whatever damage is done to the carriage will take several days to repair, five perhaps. But then after that, we must come up with something else."

"I shall think upon it, my lady," Fanny said, ever helpful and loyal. She did not have any concerns that Fanny would tattle what she was about to do to keep him at the estate.

"Thank you. We shall discuss my next move in several

days. Now run along and speak with Thomas before it grows too late."

Fanny bid her goodnight and left the room with haste. The dowager sat back in her bed, watching the flames in the grate crackle and eat the wood in its hold. Her son deserved to be happy, and there was no one more perfect for him than Princess Elena. Her friend's youngest daughter was here at Lyon Estate, and there was a reason why fate had thrown her into her son's life. It was destiny, she was sure, and now she would give fate a hand and, if not, a good shove to get her son to marry a woman who equaled him in all ways, except wealth.

*T*heo kicked the wheel of the carriage the following morning and swore. Several sprigs of the wheel were cracked. One had almost entirely broken in half.

"I do not understand how this happened. The carriage was in perfect working condition only a few days ago. How can it be that the wheel is so shot?" Theo took a calming breath, moving his attention to his lands to calm his temper, the frost burning as the morning sun moved across the grounds, making swirling mist over the fields as it rose.

This was only a small setback. In a few days, he would be able to commence his journey to London and find his wife before the creditors came and seized his home for unpaid taxes, leaving him with nothing but the title upon his head.

What would he do should the worst happen? They had a townhouse in London that was thankfully not entailed and had been part of his mother's inheritance. The home had remained in his mother's control, even after marriage.

They could go there, he supposed, even if the shame of living in London and having no country estate was better than having nowhere to go at all.

All thanks to the greedy King George. How he loathed the royal, uppity-thieving bastard.

"I apologize, my lord. When the wheel dipped into a rut on the drive, it cracked. I suppose we can be thankful that it happened here and not while the horses were in a canter."

Theo nodded, that was true, and Thomas, the stable hand, made a good point. If the wheel had broken as they were traveling at high speed, the carriage could have tipped, and the horses along with it. He could not afford to lose two of the horse stock he owned, even if they were only carriage horses.

He ran a hand through his hair. Hell, he missed having a good mount to ride. A horse he could take to town and not have to rent like he always did. The horse he rode at the estate was almost as old as he was, and she would not survive a trip to London.

"We shall have to take the wheel into the village and have it repaired. There is no other choice. See to it that it's done," Theo said, leaving the offending vehicle and wheel to the stable workers.

He strode toward the front of the house, supposing that being stuck at his home was not as bad. Better than being stranded on the side of the road, vulnerable to blackguards and highwaymen.

The sound of feminine laughter, one of them his mama's, which he had not heard in an age, caught his attention, and he glanced out onto the grounds near the estate's front, spying Miss Smith and his mother heading toward the hidden folly in the grounds.

Of course, like many features at the estate, the circular folly was as rundown and in need of repair as everything else. The new rich wife he would source would fix all that. Make it as grand and as appealing as the garden ornament had once been.

He stopped at the front of the house, watching as his mama held on to Miss Smith's arm, her animated features telling Theo she was deep in conversation and enjoying herself immensely.

Relief ran through him that he had made the right choice in the help he hired. It had been so long since she had even stepped outside. He cast a contemplative glance at the house and decided he did not need to go indoors so soon before he found his feet heading in the direction of his mother and Miss Smith.

Miss Smith...

What a surprise she was to his home. Not that he was supposed to be here long enough to know her at all, but nevertheless, today, he would not be traveling to town, so why not join his mama and her companion for a stroll? There was nothing wrong with such an activity, and it would do him good. He spent too many hours indoors, hunched over his ledgers that always came to the same amount no matter how many times he added up the figures.

Nothing.

It did not take him long to catch up to them, as they strolled at a slower pace due to his mother's health. Although, coming up to them today, he could not help but notice how well she appeared. There was a nice color to her cheeks, and her eyes were bright and alert. More so than he had seen them in a very long time.

"Good morning, ladies. I do hope you have room for

another to join you on your morning walk."

His mother halted, frowning up at him. "Why are you not on your way to London? I thought you had left this morning?" she asked him, turning to look back at the house as if that would explain his presence before her.

He turned also, watched a moment as his two footmen carried his trunks back through the front doors. He sighed.

"The carriage wheel seems to have broken. It will delay my departure a day or so, I believe. I hope you're not too disappointed that I shall be at home for two days at least."

His mother laughed, taking his arm and letting go of Miss Smith's. "I do not mind at all, my dear. Miss Smith was just telling me how much she appreciates the quiet here in Somerset. I was trying to tell her how the gardens used to be before your father ruined them all."

Theo ignored his mother's slur against his father. She had long ago blamed him for their debt, but it was not his fault. The king had cheated him in their game of cards and left the family struggling ever since. When a game was not above board or fair, one could not be blamed.

"The gardens were beautiful once. I remember as a child rows of colored beds, bees, and butterflies everywhere. The lawns on several locations about the estate slope, and I often rolled down them." And one day, he would have his children do the same once he found his rich bride and married her.

He caught the eye of Miss Smith. Her wistful smile tugged at something inside his chest. He wanted his wife to look so when she gazed over the grounds. When she helped him bring back the estate to what it once was.

Not that he would not spoil his wife, for he would. He was determined to be loving and give her everything that she desired, including a marchioness coronet.

"The estate is beautiful, even if it is a little wild and untamed. I could find myself quite happy here, whatever the season," Miss Smith said, continuing with their walk.

It was a forward statement since she was only to stay here for four weeks, the time he wanted to be away in London. She was so very sure of herself. Not that he knew many companions, but he did not think all of them were so confident and capable of speaking so before a lord of the realm.

Even so, it pleased him that she appreciated his home, no matter the condition. "I hope your stay is enjoyable, Miss Smith." They came across the stone bridge that crossed the large artificial lake his great-grandfather had dug out by hand. The circular folly was barely visible through the foliage on the hill that it sat upon.

It did not take them long to come to the base of the old gravel path that led up to the building. His mother stopped, seating herself on a small stone seat that sat under a tree. "I shall sit here and wait for you to return. I cannot walk up to the folly these days, but I can see you most of the way. It will be fine for you to continue," she said, opening up her parasol and making herself comfortable.

Theo gestured for Miss Smith to precede him, and with a little hesitation, she started up the slight incline. It had been several weeks since he had been here, and the path was starting to be almost unpassable in places from overgrown cherry trees and brambles.

He would, of course, have his gardener attend to the mess if he had one. He inwardly cringed, wishing that his circumstances were better, even before a lady's companion such as Miss Smith.

How very fortunate he was that she was not a lady of influence or society.

CHAPTER 5

*E*lena started up the hill, the incline not too bad and nothing she had not attempted before. However, the path was littered with weeds and tumbled stones that had fallen from the hillside, making it difficult to keep one's footing secure.

The vegetation had not had a good pruning for several years in her estimation, and it was not the first time she had seen the dilapidated condition of Lyon Estate.

There was little doubt in her mind that the sole reason for his lordship to travel to London for a month was to find a wife, and a rich one at that. Such unions were made every day, but it was certainly not the type of marriage she wanted for herself. It was bad enough fortune hunters saw her as a step to the top of society and nothing more.

She wanted a marriage of affection and love, like her sisters were fortunate enough to find. It did not matter whether he was a lord or merely a mister, so long as he loved and adored her.

To marry for wealth and connections appeared a cold

thing to do, and she had seen many such unions in the royal court in Atharia, many of them unhappy ones.

"How are you enjoying your time here in the country? Have you traveled much working as a lady's companion?"

Lord Lyon's voice, a little lost of breath, pulled her from her thoughts, and she glanced over her shoulder to answer. "This is the first time I've been out of London, my lord." She was not about to tell him she had traveled extensively on the continent, being who she was, she had visited most countries in Europe, just not the farmland of England.

But this was her first time in Somerset, so she wasn't too dishonest with her answer. "The estate and grounds are vast and lovely. I hope to take the dowager outside more often if this lovely weather holds."

"I would never argue with such an opinion on my lands," Lord Lyon said with a small chuckle. "The English weather, however, is likely to change at any moment. I hope it remains fine for your stay with us."

"So do I." They walked a little farther along until they came to a clearing that overlooked the grounds below. From this vantage point, they could see the dowager, shading her eyes and watching their progress. "If I may be so bold, my lord, I'm hoping you will give me permission to take some of your books from the library to my room to read. I find it difficult to sleep, and reading always helps."

His lordship cleared his throat, his attention somewhere in the direction of his home that they could see the roofline of peeping through the trees. "Of course, you may make free use of the house and everything in it. There is a music room on the ground floor if you're able to play. I feel I must warn you the piano has not been tuned for some years, but it will play well enough, I'm sure."

She studied him a moment. He appeared pensive, somewhat disappointed by his words, and she could not help but wonder if he was ashamed of the condition of his home.

Something had occurred in his lordship's life that had placed them in such dire financial straits, but what? The late Marquess of Lyon had passed several years ago, but could he have left them with such crippling debt? They had no money. That was obvious, so someone must have been the culprit, the inciting member of the family to bring that situation about.

His lordship took a deep breath, and Elena regarded his profile. He was a handsome man. Tall, athletic in build, broad shoulders, and chiseled jaw. She had the overwhelming desire to touch his face and see if the shadow that kissed his cheeks was prickly and would tickle her palm.

What would a kiss from such a man feel like?

A shiver stole through her, an odd, fluttery sensation she had never felt before, and she frowned. She should not be thinking about his lordship in such a way at all.

He was soon to London, and she was here to take care of her dearest mama's friend who needed support. His lordship would marry a rich wife and save his family's financial woes.

You could marry him. You are an heiress too.

Elena dismissed the thought as soon as she had it. She wasn't ready for marriage yet. She had only just turned nineteen, and no one she had met so far in London had interested her more than sharing pleasantries.

Lord Lyon may very well be handsome, but she did not know his personality, what his likes and dislikes were. She may not find him at all attractive if she found out he disliked cats or mistreated his horses.

She bit her lip, knowing she should not imagine anything to do with his lordship. By the time she did return to town, he would be off the marriage mart, so her mulling over him was pointless.

"Shall we continue?" he asked her.

"Yes." Elena turned to carry on just as her foot slipped on a loose rock. She stuck out her hands, bracing for the fall to come when arms wrapped about her waist quicker than she ever thought possible, and she was hauled up against the hardened, muscular chest of Lord Lyon.

She gasped, his arm embarrassingly close to the base of her breasts. Her heart beat fast, and she closed her eyes briefly. The sensation of a man holding her so close, closer than she had ever been with anyone in her life, sent a delicious tremor to flow through her blood.

He was everything a gentleman ought to be, helpful when one was going to fall, and so very lovely to lean up against after the fact.

She cleared her throat. "Thank you, my lord. I think I have my footing once again."

He eased her out of his hold, ensuring she was indeed secure on her feet. "Do you wish to return or continue? The folly is worth seeing, and the view is even better than this one. But if you are injured, we can start back down."

"I wish to continue," she admitted, turning back and starting up the hill and hoping he did not notice the warmth burning on her cheeks. She had never been so close to a man before. Not even when her uncle had her locked up in Atharia was she manhandled so.

The climb to the folly took several more minutes, a particular spot where brambles covered the path difficult before a grassy verge opened up around the folly. They climbed the stairs to walk about its circular edge, giving them a magnificent view of the estate.

Lord Lyon stopped, and Elena joined him, taking in the view. "Beautiful," she declared. It was one of the prettiest vistas she had ever seen in her life. And that was saying much since she adored Atharia and knew to her very soul that nothing would surpass the beauty of her homeland.

Somerset, however, was coming in a very close second. The estate from this height was clear to see in the valley below—the home's windows reflecting in the morning sun. The layout of the grounds was easier to make out from here too, and Elena could see the design, the rectangular and circular beds that were once filled with flowers and small hedges.

How pretty it must have been, and how terrible for his lordship and his mama not to have a pretty garden to enjoy.

"Thank you. I'm pleased that you found the climb worth your time, Miss Smith."

"I will have to come here again, I think. I would like to sketch the house from this view if you're willing to allow me. I shall gift it to your mama since she is no longer able to make it up to the folly."

Lord Lyon met her eye, and something in his dark-blue orbs made her curious. What was he thinking? Did he like her suggestion? Did it please him?

She hoped that her gesture would please, but as to why she could not say. Only that she felt for this family, their circumstances, had her uncle succeeded in becoming King of Atharia, a similar fate could have been hers and her sisters'.

They would not have had a home and would have relied on the charity and support of other royal households around Europe and England.

"That is very kind of you, Miss Smith. My mother would adore such a gift." He paused, shifting on his feet. "You seem to get along well with my mother. When you first met, I did not think you would last more than a day."

Elena had wondered that too, but the dowager, knowing who she was, the bond with her mother, had helped to smooth over a new friendship. Not that she could tell his lordship such truths, for he would ship her back off to London faster than she could pack her trunk.

"The dowager is a wonderful lady, and I knew that once she came to know me, we would get along well. I like nothing more than helping people and no matter how long your time in London takes you, my lord, know that I shall do all that I can to make my time here in Somerset most enjoyable for the dowager."

His lordship smiled, and Elena fought to school her features. The man was too handsome, too kind and sweet and available when she was determined not to be.

She swallowed, realization striking her hard that he was unlike anyone she had met so far in England. A little niggle of annoyance settled on her shoulders that she had left London and would not be there to get to know him better as equals. Had she met him in her true identity, maybe he could have been a gentleman worth getting to know better.

Here in Somerset, he thought her a lady's companion, no more than a glorified servant really. He would never look at her as a possible wife. Certainly not when he needed funds for his estate, and he would assume she had no dowry.

If only he knew she had a great deal more than just a dowry.

"Thank you. That is a great comfort to me. My mother has not had it easy since my father passed." He sighed, running a hand through his hair and making her mouth dry. "No one here has in truth. Times are difficult, which is why it's imperative that I return to town and soon."

Without thinking, Elena reached out and squeezed his lordship's arm in comfort. His eyes widened in shock, and she ripped her hand back. What was she doing? She could not touch him. Not as Miss Smith in any case. She would be lucky if she remained in her position at all, being so tactile. "I do apologize, my lord. I only meant to offer you support. I understand your need to return to town, and I wish you all the very best with your endeavors."

He did not say anything, merely nodded and looked back out over the estate, a muscle working hard in his jaw.

Elena scuttled past him, wanting to return to the dowager and quickly before she did anything else inappropriate with his lordship.

What had addled her mind that she thought to touch him? Such actions were not acceptable. Silly, naïve chit. He would think she was trying her wiles on him, which she was not.

Her royal upbringing meant she always showed comfort and support when others needed it, no matter their station.

She had to remember she could not do that here, not with Lord Lyon, who did not know the truth of her situation like the dowager did.

What a mess of things she had made, and it was only her first day. She needed to do better, and tomorrow when he left, she would. That she could promise him above all else.

CHAPTER 6

*L*ater that evening, Theo sat at his desk, running through the figures once again, trying to squeeze out any available funds for his upcoming trip to London. Not to mention the carriage wheel that he needed to pay the repairs for.

He slammed the financial tome closed. There was no use, he could not grow money on trees, and there would be no loose change about the house. He would have to travel to London and wear the same attire he had commissioned for himself two years prior.

His footman would act as his valet. A position young Sam had been taking up since his previous valet had passed away not long ago.

The tinkling sound of pianoforte keys met his ears, and he leaned back in his chair and closed his eyes. It had been so many years since he'd heard the ivory notes sing through the house. His mother had not played long before his father had died. He had often wondered if his parents were as happy as he had always thought them. He did not believe they were.

But what he did know was, right at this moment, the sound of lively music was just what he needed. A little light in his dark world, a small reminder that there were still pretty things to enjoy. That there were still days ahead of him to look forward to.

Miss Smith was an excellent player, and he had little doubt it was she who made the pianoforte sing.

Theo stood and went to the door in the library that joined the music room and opened it a fraction. He watched as Miss Smith played with a proficiency of a master, her long, delicate fingers moving over the keys with grace and ability.

He was fortunate in his choice of companion for his mama, and he was certain he was leaving his parent in capable hands.

"You play very well, Miss Smith," he said, unable to remain hidden for long. Such playing required compliments, and it would be good practice for when he went to town to find a wife. He noted she did not start, nor did her fingers falter when she recognized his presence. A master indeed.

"I was taught from a young age, my lord. Your mama wanted to hear some music in the house as she has retired for the night. She assured me she would be able to hear the music from her room. I hope I did not interrupt you, however."

He waved her concerns away, savoring the sight of her before him. How lovely it was to have company, an intelligent, capable woman under the roof that was not family. Miss Smith had changed into a light-blue gown, reminding him of a clear summer day's sky. She was a beautiful woman, and he needed to remind himself that she was not for him. Not even when she watched him as she played, a small smile about her sweet lips.

Lips that begged to be kissed, to savor and taste at every opportunity known to man.

"Music played by capable hands is never an impediment. My mother is correct. It is very enjoyable to hear the music in the home." Miss Smith continued to play, changing flawlessly into another song, another composer.

She bit her lip through a difficult passage, and his heart stuttered. What was wrong with him? He should not be admiring her so. Hell, he needed to return to London to gain a rich wife and disregard his wayward thoughts on the lady before him.

"I'm happy that you enjoy my playing. I will make sure to do it often while I'm here if it will please your mama."

For a time, Theo could not remove himself, although he ought. She was an unmarried maid, his mother's companion, and he was a lord of marriageable age. Should he be caught here with her, she would be compromised. That he could not marry her to save her reputation, he would forever be judged as a scoundrel who seduced an innocent woman.

Even so, his feet refused to budge. He lost himself in the notes, admiring how she moved and flowed with the music. The pianoforte had not been tuned for years, but it still played well and sounded divine.

He had missed nights such as these. To spend a few moments not worrying about how he would pay his staff, keep roofs over his tenants' heads, and his mama healthy.

He could not fail any of them. He had to marry well, as unpalatable as that future seemed. Marrying a woman for her fortune had never been what he had wanted, but it was unfortunately something that he had to do.

The song came to an end, and Miss Smith dropped her hands into her lap from the keys, a pleased smile tilting her lips.

He clapped, his appreciation heartfelt. "Marvelous, Miss Smith. If my mother does not, I command you to play each evening, even if I am not here. Your playing is insurmountable."

A light blush kissed her cheeks. He could not stop admiring her charm and warm personality, unlike anyone he had ever met before. He hoped whoever the woman was whom he married would be similar.

She slipped from the chair and stood before him, dipping into a curtsy. "I will, of course, my lord. Now, I had better go upstairs and check on your mama before I retire."

Theo stepped out of her way and allowed her to pass. He looked over his shoulder, watching her leave. There was an elegance to her, a grace he could not understand. What had been her upbringing? Why was it she was a lady's companion and not some gentleman's wife?

He turned back to the pianoforte, frowning down at it in thought. Perhaps like him, Miss Smith had secrets too and was trying to make the best of her life just as he was.

He could only hope they would both succeed with their endeavors.

*E*lena took a calming breath as she reached the base of the stairs. With Lord Lyon watching her play piano, she had been fraught with nerves. How she had managed the difficult pass of Bach she would never know. It had been a long time since she had allowed anyone to hear her play.

Before their uncle had attempted his coup, she had played often in Atharia, for her family and the royal court. But it had been two years at least since she had done so. Her uncle had deemed her playing inept and had made her play before him and the court, for hours, all the while snarling and throwing out insults at her ability.

She had come to loathe the instrument, and yet she should not have. She should have directed all her loathing and hate to her uncle. That his lordship appreciated her playing was a soothing balm to an injured soul in need of repair.

She had watched him take pleasure in the music. For a moment, he had closed his eyes, reveling in her playing, and she thought she might swoon from the temptation he made. A small, mischievous smile had tweaked his lips, and she could not stop thinking of what he would be like to kiss.

An absurd, silly thought she did not need to have, not when he was about to go to town and find a wife. And certainly not while she was here, living in his house as a lady's companion and lying to him about it all.

What if he sees you in London after his wedding? What will you do then?

Elena raced to the dowager's rooms, peeking into the door and glad to see she was abed but still awake. She knocked on the door, and the marchioness waved her in.

"What is it, my dear? You do seem pale. Is everything well?" her ladyship asked her, patting the blankets at her side.

Elena closed the door and went to the bed, seating herself beside the dowager. "It has just occurred to me that in the future, when I return to London, that Lord Lyon may see me there. That he will think I'm a companion attending balls and parties that I should not be attending. What shall I do then? What should I do now about this problem that I did not think about?"

Elena nibbled her bottom lip. Mayhap she had not thought about her plan to hide in the country all that well after all.

Her ladyship chuckled. "Never fear, my dear. We shall tell my son the truth of your situation when you're to leave. That is all we can do. I shall make up some excuse for your disguise, but once he knows I was friends with your dear mama, he will not question you being here. He will merely think the disguise was to enable you to be incognito in the country. Safe from gossips, and that you sought his house as a refuge to enable that."

Elena hoped that would be the case, but what if it was not? "But will he not be angry? He hired me, and although all of that was by design and above board, I do not want him to be angry. I do not want him to think badly of me," she admitted truthfully. And she did not. Somehow in the last two days that she had known Lord Lyon, she had come to respect him and his choices. She wanted him to feel the same about her.

"He will not be angry. He rarely loses his temper. My son is incapable of being insulted. He will be honored to have helped you. Now, if you were part of the English royal family, I may have concerns for your standing when it came to my son, but you're from foreign shores. He will not judge you. I'm certain of that."

Elena hoped that was true, for she did not want to create a scandal or cause any embarrassment for his lordship. Not here in Somerset or back in London.

"If you're certain," she hedged, hating the idea of his lordship being so upset with her for lying to him that he would no longer treat her with kindness. The year with her uncle had hurt, and she did not think she could stand a bad word from anyone ever again. Not during her entire life.

"I am very certain, my dear. Now, run along and get some rest. I'm hoping to walk in the gardens again tomorrow and maybe visit the river that I have not sat beside in some months."

Elena was unsure why she did what she did next, but she leaned over and kissed her ladyship's forehead. "Good-night, my lady. I look forward to our adventures on the morrow."

"Good night, my dear," her ladyship stated as Elena stood and started for the door, a pleased smile on the dowager's lips.

Elena strode to her room, her steps slow as she thought over her ladyship's words and her son, who occupied too much space in her head. As if materializing him from her constant thoughts, she heard the handle of a door at the opposite end of the passage and turned, catching his lordship retiring for the night.

She ought to go to her room, and yet, she stood there, observing him, stupefied by his very presence. Her heart beat fast, rattling against her ribs, and a fluttering lifted in her belly.

This was bad. She should not lust over her employer, for that was what he was to her right now. Her silly plan had enabled that ruse, but now she did not want to play the role of companion, not when it came to his lordship. She sighed, her ruse unable to be changed, not now at least. She wasn't here to win the heart of the man down the hall from her. She was here to look after her ladyship and return to her life in four weeks. If he was still unattached then, maybe he could make his interest known.

Lord Lyon glanced down the hall, and their eyes met, held. He watched her a moment, heat searing her skin as his attention slid over her like a physical touch. His eyes taking in her every feature, her dress right down to her silk slippers before traveling back to her face. Her breathing increased, and she shivered, wishing it were more than his eyes considering her flesh.

His lordship stepped back and closed the door, the snip of the lock putting paid to her wayward thoughts.

Her sisters would rip her limbs from her body if they knew she harbored such sinful, ruinous thoughts. She bit her lip. Well, Holly would, at least. Alessa may smirk and congratulate her on becoming a woman she could admire.

With that thought, Elena ran the rest of the way to her room, shut the door with a determined slam, and locked it too. She wasn't sure if it were to keep his lordship out or herself locked in.

CHAPTER 7

The few staff at Lyon Estate had set up a lovely blanket and picnic basket for her ladyship and Elena to enjoy the following day. With the carriage wheel still being fixed in town, Elena knew the marquess was still about at the estate, and a luncheon down by the river was just what she needed to ensure she kept away from his lordship and his wicked looks that had kept her up half the night.

Heat crept over her cheeks at the thought of how she had acted the evening before. Whatever would he think of her? Some light skirt, she was sure, a lady's companion who was after a lord and forward enough to watch him seek his room for the night?

She was none of those things, but what had possessed her to stand in the passage last evening and ogle his lordship? The stupidity of her actions was beyond her.

However would she face him when she had to today?

Thankfully her ladyship broke her fast in her room this morning, and so Elena was not required to breakfast downstairs, but having not eaten anything due to her nerves over what she had done, now she was ravenous.

Her stomach rumbled as if reminding her of her lack of sustenance. She poured a glass of Madeira for both her ladyship and herself, downing hers before she handed the glass to her ladyship.

"Here you are, my lady. I shall serve lunch now if you're ready."

"Serve away, my dear. I'm ready, although the idea of a princess serving a marchioness is preposterous."

Elena chuckled, handing her ladyship a sweet biscuit that was topped with jam. "If pretending to be someone else enables me some peace, even for a month, I would not mind feeding a bug."

Her ladyship chewed her food, studying her a moment. "I cannot help but think, my dear, that you would suit my son. Now I know you're not looking to marry just yet, and you wish to remain here for some respite, and I support that of course," her ladyship stated, reaching out to pat her hand. "But he is eligible, and I do believe he is curious about you. Mayhap you ought to tell him the truth now and see if a union between you two may be something that would blossom and grow."

The memory of his lordship's heated gaze the evening before materialized in her mind, and she would be a liar if she thought the idea had not occurred to her too. But she could not. A love match was not forced simply because she was here and eligible and wealthy enough to save the estate. "I want to be courted and fallen in love with, my lady. I do not want to marry because I'm eligible. I respect your son, and he is a very attractive man, but I would prefer for my union to happen naturally and without any assistance or pressure from anything else, if you understand. I hope I have not offended you."

"Of course not," her ladyship stated. "But I am fond of you, and I know your mama would approve of our families joining at last. But I shall step back, allow you to have your time, and find love when love is ready to capture your heart. My son, as you say, is off to London, most probably tomorrow, and I shall look forward to whoever captures his attention to be the next Marchioness of Lyon. I will certainly be glad to release the occupation as soon as he announces his betrothal."

Elena sipped her drink, taking in their surroundings, the river that flowed slowly before them, the few ducks she could see in the reeds across the other side. They sat under the shade of a large oak, but even in the shadows, the day was uncommonly warm.

"Have you ever swam here, my lady? There looks to be a sandy verge leading out to the lake here. It's very tempting. I must say," Elena said, the corset and shift under her gown a little sticky from the heat.

"I have not swum here since Theo was a little boy, but I believe Theo still swims here in the summer. You are more than welcome to, if it pleases you. No one ever comes down in this part of the garden."

The idea was enticing to sneak away and swim later today when her ladyship took her afternoon rest. "His lordship would not mind if I swam here through the day? I'm supposed to be looking after you, not galloping about the estate as if I'm here enjoying a house party."

"No, not at all." The dowager laughed, plopping a strawberry into her mouth. "He will have me to answer to if he does, for if I wish for my companion to enjoy a relaxing afternoon swim, that is up for me to decide."

Elena looked back at the clear, blue water, the sight of it more tempting than even his lordship was right at this moment. "Then I think I shall. Thank you for being so lovely and kind to me."

The dowager reached out and patted her cheek. "My pleasure, my dear. Now do be a doll and pass me another one of those biscuits. They are divine."

Elena did so and changed the conversation to his lordship's trip and who she knew to be in town and possible matches for the marquess. The conversation kept her ladyship occupied, but Elena's mind was elsewhere. All she could think about was cooling off in the waters behind her, sooner rather than later, if the oppressive heat became any worse.

*L*ater that afternoon, Elena snuck out of the house through the terrace doors on the eastern side and ran toward the bank of the river, where she'd sat at lunch with the marchioness.

With few servants, no one had noticed her departure, and with his lordship having traveled to the nearby village to check on the carriage wheel, it was safe enough to go for a swim.

Elena stripped off her light muslin gown, stays, stockings, and boots, leaving only her shift. She would have to wash and dry it later today, but the shift would have to do as swimming attire with nothing else to use.

She flexed her toes in the warm, soft grass before making her way down to the river's edge, dipping one foot into the water. It was cool, but not too cold that one could not swim comfortably.

Elena looked over her shoulder, checking to see she was

indeed alone before stepping onto the sandy bank beneath the water's edge. The cooling sensation instantly made her feel better, and she walked farther out, each step bringing her ever closer to bliss.

She dived in when it was safe enough to do so, the water refreshing and chill against her heated skin. She laughed, unable to hold back the glee within her that she was here. That she was in Somerset, away from the *ton*, and the pressures her title brought her. That she was swimming in a river at a country estate, unseen due to being a companion and free to do what she liked, was utter joy.

She could not help but feel this trip to Lyon Estate was one of her finest ideas to date, and she was a little proud of herself for doing what she did. She dived into the water again to celebrate.

*T*heo walked the three miles from town, having opted to leave the carriage horses in their stalls on this hot summer's day. The tree-lined river that ran through his property beckoned him, and before he had thought too much about it, he had untied his cravat and stuffed it into his pocket.

He pulled his shirt from his breeches. His coat was already hanging over his arm, him having discarded that a mile or so ago.

He made his way through the copse of trees, the sound of splashing making his steps falter. Theo heard the noise again and proceeded with caution just in case some of the female servants were cooling off on this hot day.

He came into a clearing that revealed the lake, and the sight that met his eyes sent ice through his veins. A woman was swimming, but something was wrong. Her legs were flailing above the water, but little else.

Theo bolted through the trees, discarding his clothes somewhere in the bushes in his haste to get to her. He ran and dove to where she was, his breeches still on, along with his boots.

He caught her about the waist, and beneath the water, he could hear her scream the last of her breath in fear. Her hand was caught in weeds, their immovable talons wrapping about her wrist and arm.

He wrenched at the weed, ripping it from the murky, muddy ground, and clasped the woman about the waist, pushing up from the bottom of the lake.

They burst from the water and surprise and fear shot through his blood at the realization of whom he held. Miss Smith coughed and sputtered in her attempt to gain her breath. He swam them back to the sandy verge before lifting her into his arms and carrying her to the river's bank.

He laid her down, and she rolled to the side, gasping for air. Theo gave her a moment, deciding to rub her back in comfort instead of asking her what she was doing at the lake all alone without someone keeping watch.

Had he not come past when he did, she would have drowned. The idea made him want to cast up his accounts at just how close she was to not being here anymore.

"Miss Smith, can you talk? How are you feeling?" he asked her, pleased to see that she was coughing less and her breathing was calming. He pushed her hair off her face, mud from the bottom of the lake across her jaw.

Theo rubbed it away with his thumb, hating the idea that she could have had a watery grave had he not found her in time.

She rolled onto her back, staring up at the cloudless sky. "Thank you, my lord. I do not know what happened. I was swimming, and then I got caught and did not have the strength to push away from the reeds." A shiver stole over her, and he noted for the first time what she was wearing. Or at least, the lack of clothing that she wore. Nothing but her shift, which was as transparent as the glass on a window.

He reached up and clasped her gown, laying it over her. "You should never swim alone. Promise me that you will not do so again."

She nodded, leaning upon her elbows, watching him with something akin to awe. "You saved my life. I owe you everything," she stated, a little surprise in her tone.

He slumped back on his ass, relief pouring through him that she seemed well and not harmed. "Yes, but I would prefer not to have to attempt such a rescue again if you do not mind. Promise me, Miss Smith, that you will never swim alone."

Her attention shifted to the river, and she contemplated it a moment. "I can promise you that I shall never, not here or anywhere else, ever swim alone again, my lord."

Her declaration pleased him. It was one less thing he had to worry about. "I assume with you being out here on your own that my mother is having her afternoon rest?"

She nodded, sitting up and wrapping her arms about her knees. "She is. We had a picnic here today, and she suggested I swim here this afternoon. I should have thought about the danger of swimming alone and brought a maid with me."

He sighed, moving to sit beside her, doubting that had a maid been here, she would have been any safer in the water. The maid would have most likely frozen in fear, panicked, and Miss Smith would have drowned in any case.

"Never mind," he found himself saying, giving her a consoling look. She was shivering now, her lips blue, her teeth chattering. Theo spied his coat dropped on the ground not far from where he dove into the lake and stood to fetch it, coming back and laying it over her shoulders.

She snuggled into his apparel, and the sight of her, disheveled, shaken, but relieved, sent an odd desire of protection through him. He wanted to keep Miss Smith safe, give her comfort, but why he could not fathom.

Mayhap her almost drowning today had discombobulated his mind as well, and he was in need of a stiff toddy.

"I should return you to the house. I think a warm bath and a brandy might be just the thing that you require, Miss Smith."

"Elena, please, my lord. After the service you rendered me today, I think calling me so formally is no longer a requirement." She stood, wobbling, and he clasped her hand, helping to steady her.

"Come, we shall leave now and return you to your rooms. I can fetch a doctor if you think you're in need of one."

She shook her head, the last of her pins holding up her hair falling to the ground. She had long, dark locks that were tangled, and in places had little specks of moss from the river. He would suggest to the maid attending her that her hair required a thorough washing and brushing.

"No, I am well. I'm merely a little shaken by the event, that is all. I thank you for your kindness."

"Of course, but if you change your mind, do send word. The doctor lives in the village nearby and can be here within the half-hour."

She threw him a tentative smile. "I will let you know should my condition change, my lord."

He nodded, helping her navigate his overgrown lawn as they made their way closer to the estate. His mother stood on the terrace, a concerned frown between her brows when she noticed their wet apparel and unkempt appearance.

She started toward them, and Theo held up a hand to stop her progress. They were almost at the terrace themselves, no need for his mama to attempt the steps without help and injure herself too. He did not need to save any more ladies today from self-harm. Miss Smith, Elena as he preferred to think of her from now on, had filled his quota well enough.

CHAPTER 8

*E*lena woke with a start, the bed wet with sweat, her face damp with tears. She swiped at her cheeks, the nightmare vivid and all too real still in her mind. She threw back the sheets she was sleeping under and sat at the edge of the bed. For a moment, she took deep, calming breaths, trying to settle her racing heart.

She closed her eyes, the murky, green water of the river materialized in her mind. The sound of her heart in her ears as it grew ever panicked at her predicament. The thought of drowning and not being able to breathe ever again, of dying in a watery grave. Her screams that no one would hear.

And then Lord Lyon, his strong arms clasping her and wrenching her free, his body hard up against her back as he swam her to the surface.

Elena stood and strode to the door, pulling it open without thought to how much noise she made. She needed a stiff drink, stronger than brandy. A good whisky would do, but where to find one?

The house was quiet at this time of the night. The

servants long to bed. Using the moonlight, she headed for the staircase and the library downstairs, where she knew his lordship kept his liquor.

The home's downstairs was as soundless as the first floor, and she made little effort to remain silent in this part of the house. No one would be about, and she was quite safe.

She pushed open the library door and skidded to a stop at the sight of Lord Lyon, bent over his desk and sound asleep on a stack of ledgers, his candle flickering as the wick was succumbing to the wax.

For a moment, she debated whether she should leave him be or see if he was well. He really ought to go to bed. Sleeping on one's desk would never achieve a good outcome for the following day.

But it was not her place to tell him what to do or intrude on his privacy.

He did appear utterly adorable tousled, and asleep. She stepped closer, unable to help herself, and peeked at him a little closer.

His hand sat under his face, and his eyelashes were longer than she had thought them. They fanned out over his cheeks, reminding her of her own dark hair and eyes.

Before she knew what she was doing, she reached out, shaking his shoulder just the smallest amount. "My lord? Wake up," she suggested to him. She kneeled at his side, bringing herself far closer than she ought to be. "My lord? You really ought to sleep in your bed. This would not be helping your neck in the slightest," she prattled on, hoping the sound of her voice, not so much her words, would wake him without a start.

His eyes fluttered, settled on her, and her stomach clenched as his attention did not shift.

"Elena?" he asked. The sound of her name on his lips, honeyed and guttural with sleep, was not what she needed to hear. Her name had never sounded so evocative in her life.

"My lord, you have fallen asleep on your desk."

Slowly, he became aware of where he was and what had happened. He sat up, taking in his surroundings, just as the candle guttered them into the moonlight and nothing else.

The change in atmosphere was instant. Elena's stomach trembled, she should not be here with his lordship, but then she hadn't known he was going to be in the room at all when she came down to get a whisky.

"What are you doing here?" he asked her, relighting the candle before twisting around to face her. Elena realized she was still kneeling before him and quickly stood. The stack of papers he had on his desk hit her hip, and before she could reach for them, they tumbled onto the floor.

"I'm so sorry," she professed, kneeling once again to pick them up. Lord Lyon joined her, helping her to pick up the mess. Heat kissed her cheeks, and she was thankful for the dark, so he could not see her embarrassment.

"Lord save me," she thought she heard him mumble. His hands halted stacking papers, and she glanced at him, frowning.

"Is something wrong, my lord?" she asked, uncertain of what was going on.

His swallow was almost audible. "Your gown, Miss Smith," he murmured, back to formalities once again. He turned his face away, the muscle in his jaw working before he said, "it is gaping."

Elena felt her mouth fall open before she took in her nightdress and gasped, clutching underclothes to her body.

In her haste for a nightcap, she had not put on her dressing gown or bothered to pick up a shawl. The shift she slept in, silky and one of the prettiest underclothes she had brought, was gaping at her bosom and giving his lordship a perfect view of her breasts.

His gaze scorched her skin, and heat prickled down her spine. "I'm so sorry, my lord. I came down for a nightcap after a disturbing dream. I know I should not have, and I found you. I did not think you would be here, and then I woke you. I've made a mess of your desk. Please do not think that I am in any way trying to seduce you. I'm here to do a job, and that is all. I'm here to look after your dearest mama and nothing else."

He reached out, clamping her mouth closed with his fingers, halting the words that spewed out of her mouth. She did not know whether to be thankful for his intervention or offended he had touched her person.

Not that she minded him touching her person in truth. His hungry gaze of just before, well, she could get used to a man, her husband, looking at her so. It made her feel odd and desirable. Both emotions an elixir to her after so many months of feeling nothing at all but boredom.

"You had a nightmare? Did you want to talk about it?" he asked. He reached out, taking her hand and helping her to stand. He took the few papers he held and placed them on his desk before leading her over to a settee before the unlit hearth.

Elena watched as he poured them both a whisky before handing her a good-sized portion.

"Drink this, and you will sleep better. I promise."

Elena did as he asked, reveling in the warmth of the amber liquid as it slid down her throat. She sighed, supposing she ought to tell him since he asked. "I dreamed

I was drowning again, and I woke up in a panic. I did not think that anyone else may be about, and I should have. I do apologize for intruding on you in such a way."

He sipped his drink, settling beside her on the settee and watching the unlit hearth as if it were roaring with flames.

"It is understandable that you would dream about the event. You are very lucky to be alive. Should I not have come along when I did, I do not even want to think about what would have happened."

Not could, but would. Life was so precious. His lordship's words reminded Elena that she had promised herself to live after her uncle had been removed from power, to make each day count. She had not lived up to that promise of late. In fact, she had failed herself miserably.

"I would have died," Elena stated, for it was the truth. Lord Lyon saved her, and she owed him her life. "Thank you, truly, for saving me. I cannot remember if I stated such back at the river, but now, seeing you here, I most certainly will make that statement." She downed the rest of her drink, so very thankful she was in the library of Lord Lyon's estate, breathing and speaking to him.

"Try and not dwell on it, Elena. It will not do you any good. The outcome today was a fortunate one, and that is all. I'm glad I was there to help."

She turned and watched him. He continued to stare at the hearth, but then, sensing her interest, he met her gaze, and the movement felt like a physical touch.

She swallowed the need that rose within her, the want for the man beside her. She hardly knew his lordship. How could she want him as much as she did? Was it some debt she thought she owed him for saving her?

No. No, she knew that was not what made her insides

jump and sizzle. It was the man himself. There was something about him that called to her. From the moment she had met him, she knew he was kind, a gentleman to his core. Never had she reacted to a man in such a way. And now, she could not do anything about it. She was here as a companion, not to try to win his love and hand in marriage.

"In any case, I will say it one last time. Thank you, my lord." Elena stood and ignored the disappointment that crossed his features when she did so. Her time away from London was precious, a time to take stock and restore herself. Should his lordship return from London unmarried still, then perhaps she could show him her hand and reveal who she really was. Mayhap they could then see what may happen between them, but not now. She would not allow herself to fall into his lordship's arms and then watch as he rode off and married someone else. Nor would she tell him the truth. That she was an heiress, capable of saving him, everything and everyone on the property from the debt that crippled it, merely to have him ask for her hand after the fact. How would she ever know he loved her, not her title and money?

She would never know if his love was true if he knew she was a princess.

"Goodnight, my lord," she said, determined not to look back at his lordship.

"Goodnight, Miss Smith," he replied, just as she closed the door and left all thoughts of his lordship locked away in the library. She could only hope now that is where they would stay for the remainder of her time here and not wiggle back into her mind and drive her to distraction.

Or worse, straight into his arms.

CHAPTER 9

Theo stood in the stable the following morning and could not believe what Thomas, the stable hand, was explaining to him. "I'm sorry, but the horse is what?" Theo asked again, needing to hear it a second time to be sure he had heard correctly.

"One of the carriage horses has turned out lame this morning, my lord. You have the other, of course, but he is getting on in age, and I would not recommend traveling to London without the other mount."

Theo ran a hand through his hair, walking up to the stall where the horse was stabled. The stall was small to limit movement, but full of hay to pad the horse's sore hoof.

"I cannot travel to London without having them both in pristine condition." With neither carriage horse able to leave, he supposed he could take his mount, but he doubted she would survive the journey either, as old as she was.

This was a disaster. He needed to return to town to find a wife, or the estate would be lost, surrendered to

The Crown for debts he could not pay. He could not allow anyone to take more from him than they already had.

"How long do you think it will take for the horse to heal? Is the lameness severe, or do you believe just a slight sprain?"

Thomas leaned over the stall door, studying the horse who stared at them both as if wondering what all the tension was about. "A week perhaps, mayhap less. I do think it's only a small sprain, nothing too much wrong with him. But rest is what he needs, and I would suggest putting off your trip to London for a week at most."

A week! Hell, he may as well put it off indefinitely. It would mean he would miss the Levingstone ball, a night where he knew many of his acquaintances had met their wives since the ball attracted the richest and most eligible young women in London.

"Well, I suppose there is little I can do," he said, turning to face the two footmen who had followed him to the stable, expecting to leave with him for London. "Return my trunks to my room. We will not be traveling to town until next week."

The young men did as he bade, and Theo strode from the stable, needing air and a brisk stroll before returning indoors. How was he to face his mama and let her know his trip to town was postponed yet again? She was relying on him to save them all, to keep the roof over her head and everyone else's too. To ensure the people who lived and worked at Lyon Estate remained doing so for years to come, not losing their jobs because their sovereign had cheated his father at a game of cards.

"Damn royal rogue," he cursed.

He turned about the corner of the house and slammed

headlong into Miss Smith. Her breasts hit his chest, her gasp and his melding as one.

Instinctively he reached out, steadying her and stopping her from falling back. Her gloveless hands pressed up against his chest as she set herself to rights, her cheeks rosy, her eyes wide with surprise.

"Lord Lyon, I do apologize. I was woolgathering and not watching where I was going."

"No," he said, shaking his head. "It is I who should apologize. I hope you are not injured. I came about the corner without thinking that anyone else would be strolling so early in the morning."

"Oh, well, as to that," she said, holding up a square basket with a small napkin sitting atop of it. "Your cook found me in the breakfast room this morning and asked me to rush this out to you for your trip to town. I'm glad that I caught you, for I do want to wish you well and thank you again for allowing me to be here and care for your mama. I promise I shall take care of her for you."

Theo took the basket that Miss Smith, Elena held out for him, the scent of chutney and ham teasing his senses. "Thank you for bringing me my lunch, but it will no longer be necessary to wish me farewell. The horse is lame, and I cannot leave for another week at most."

"Oh, I'm so sorry," she said, her wide brown eyes drawing him in and making the harsh reality of him being stuck here in Somerset not so dreadful after all. Not when Elena was under his roof, a welcome distraction to his otherwise strained and depressing existence.

"But a week is not so very long. I'm sure the horse will be better in no time, and you shall be on your way." She moved past him, and he turned and walked beside her as they started back toward the front of the house. "Does business take you to town, or do you intend to enjoy the highlights of the Season, which, if I'm correct, is in full swing in London."

Theo thought about her question a moment, wondering how truthful he needed to be with her. Not that he needed to tell her anything, she was a lady's companion after all, and he did not need to be so open with her, but there was something about Elena that he liked and trusted and the desire to lay down all his troubles beckoned like a soothing balm.

"There is little doubt that you have noticed the estate and grounds are in a dreadful condition. My father was cheated out of some very valuable land during a card game in London several years before his death, and while we own this great estate and several thousand acres of forest, we no longer have farming land. I'm in need of a rich wife, Miss Smith. That is the truth of my situation, and the sooner I arrive in London, the sooner I shall find one who needs a marchioness coronet in exchange for saving my to let pockets."

She frowned up at him, and he could not help but wonder what she was thinking. Did she think him a pathetic gentleman landowner who did not know how to budget and live within his income? He was, of course, better than his father ever had been with budgeting, but it would have been welcome to have the income from those prized lands to keep the house and grounds from falling into disrepair. To pay his taxes.

"What does 'pockets to let' mean, my lord? I do not think I have ever heard of the expression."

He grimaced, wishing he did not need to explain. "It means that there is nothing in my pockets anymore, Miss Smith. That they are to let to anyone who can fill them with blunt. I never wished to find a wife in such a way, I would have liked to marry for affection, but it is not to be for me, unfortunately. I must think of the estate, my mother who relies on me to keep a roof over her head and a warm meal on the table each night."

Miss Smith pulled him to a stop, the touch of her hand on his arm making him yearn for things he could not have. Had he been rich enough, a woman such as Elena would have caught his attention. He had never cared about title and rank. Above all else, he prized a person's character, honesty, and integrity. Miss Smith, from what he knew of her in the three short days since she had arrived at his estate, was all those things. And beautiful too, inside and out. His mama certainly liked her very much, and she was a good judge of character.

"Surely your position can not be so grave. Is there anyone in the country that is wealthy enough that you may be able to court without leaving Somerset at all? I know a week is not so very long, but what if the horse is lame for longer than that time? What will you do then?"

He shrugged, continuing their walk and starting down the front drive, bypassing the front doors. "I suppose there is little I can do about it. I shall just have to hope the horse is not, and I can return to town next week. I do hope you do not think less of me marrying for wealth alone, Miss Smith. I feel like I have burdened you with all my concerns, and they are not yours to bear at all."

"Not at all," she said, her tone light and without censor. "I am more than aware of what expectations families place upon their children, what is expected of them. I commend you for doing what you must to secure your future. I know I should not like to lose such a home, should I risk losing one such as Lyon Estate. I do hope your trip to London happens soon and you do all that you set out to achieve, my lord."

"Thank you," Theo said, her words soothing his confused soul. To marry for money had never sat well with him, but then, as Elena said, he was not the only person who would do the same should the need arise. And his future wife, whomever that ended up being, was not coming away from this marriage with nothing.

He would dote on her, spoil her and love her, make her as happy as he could, and in time, perhaps both their emotions would become engaged, and they would find a happy medium and have a happy life.

Miss Smith dipped into a curtsy and, with a small smile, turned and walked back to the estate. He watched her go, a feeling of loss coming over him that he was making a mistake, no matter what was at risk.

To marry for money and security was no marriage at all and would only end in dissolution and regret.

He hoped he was wrong, but he could not shake the feeling that he was not and that his trip to London would be the beginning of the end, not just for the estate but for his own happiness.

CHAPTER 10

*E*lena watched from her bedroom window as Lord Lyon strode about the gardens, kicking small border stones out of the way whenever he came across one. He appeared lost and so alone, and her heart went out to him.

So much pressure on his shoulders, no matter how broad they were. With all that he had to achieve, marry well and line his pockets, the weight of what he must do was a lot to bear, especially when his lordship had stated that it was not the kind of marriage he desired.

Elena looked about her room, better than others she had seen in the home. At least in here, the silk wallpaper of exotic birds was not peeling away, exposing the plaster beneath.

The house needed thousands of pounds of repairs. The estate, from her vantage point up high in her room, had once been beautiful. The garden designs could easily be seen, the lawns, overgrown, stretched out beyond to the river and the wooded acreage that surrounded the estate.

When he married well and had his home as it once

had been, she would like to see it again, to see he was settled and happy and the estate as it should always have been.

You are rich enough to save him, have him for yourself, and marry him.

She was, she admitted, but she could not tell him now who she was. What would he think of her when she admitted she had lied to him? Played a servant, for heaven's sake, and all so that she could escape London for a month.

He would think her a spoiled, little royal brat, and there were times she had felt the same about herself. But then she remembered how much she loathed crowds, the noise and fake laughter, the false friendships and men who sought a princess, not the woman beneath all the silk and jewels.

The laughter was the worst. She could not help but feel it was aimed at her. That people were judging her whenever they found something funny, and their eyes met across a ballroom floor.

The reality of it was that they were probably not laughing at Elena at all, but after months of torment from her uncle, she could not stomach society. She could not return now to London, not when she enjoyed herself so much here in Somerset.

Lady Lyon was so pleasant and accommodating, allowing her time to roam and relax, just what she needed. She supposed it was fortunate that her ladyship had recognized her through her mama, for she had gifted her with the little holiday she needed to regroup and revitalize herself.

His lordship stared out over the grounds, hands on his hips, and she couldn't help but wonder what he was thinking. Were his thoughts as jumbled as her own? Did he think of her at all?

She had not thought of marrying anyone, certainly not while away in the country, but being here now, getting to know Lord Lyon, she could not help but contemplate a future as his marchioness.

He was kind and sweet, and he had saved her life. He would be a good husband. She was certain of that. No man who cared and loved his mother as much as he did had a mean bone in his body.

He turned and stared up at the house. Elena did not move from where she stood in the window, and she smiled when he bowed in her presence before striding off and out of sight.

The marchioness was downstairs, having decided on an afternoon tea with a nearby elderly neighbor. Elena was invited, of course, but playing the part of companion, she had cried off and allowed her ladyship to catch up with her friend alone.

Elena left her room, deciding on giving herself a tour of the home instead. The house was enormous, over one hundred rooms, she was sure, and the south wing she had not visited at all.

She walked down the passage. The farther along she went, the cooler the air in the hall became. She supposed not being lived in, the windows' furnishings were drawn and allowed little light. The doors were closed in this part of the house, and mold covered the wood paneling on the walls. The carpets were tattered and in need of replacing, and parts of ceilings were falling away.

What a dreadful state the home was in, and she could understand why Lord Lyon needed a rich wife, and yet, he would need a lady who was not only rich but immensely so to make the estate as grand as it once must have been, to return it back to its former brilliance.

"You've found my shame," a masculine voice sounded behind her.

She spun about and found his lordship standing only a few feet from her. His disillusioned gaze on the walls and floors, just as hers had been.

"I'm sorry to intrude. I thought I would give myself a tour, and I had not seen the south wing yet. I hope you do not mind," she said.

He moved past her, shaking his head. "Not at all. The house is what it is, and you know my circumstances now."

Elena moved to walk beside him as they made their way farther along the passage. They came to the end of the corridor where instead of a door, an archway led into a large room that overlooked the stables and the grounds on the south side of the estate.

Elena looked out the window, the pane of glass in need of a good wash. She spied a maze that she had not noticed before, although it too needed a good prune.

"What was this room, my lord?"

He moved farther into the space and wrenched open the drapes over several windows, and a large, rectangular ballroom appeared. Dust floated in the air as the room came into focus. Or at least, what was left of the space after years of neglect.

A fireplace sat along its center wall, gold gilding upon two cherubs that held the marble mantel in place. Large mirrors ran along the walls, opposite the windows, and Elena could imagine its beauty, the parties and dancing that the room had seen.

"There has not been a ball at the estate for twenty

years. I can only remember this room covered up and unused."

Elena walked along the parquetry floor, coming up to his lordship. "I do hope that you are able to have your home just as you wish it and how it must have been. I know I would have loved to have danced in such a room. A lady's companion could only dream of attending such an event," she lied, knowing she had danced in much grander rooms than this one, but none had been Lord Lyon's ballroom, a man whom she was starting to respect more than most.

He stared down at her with a small smile. She nibbled on the inside of her lip, her mind a whirl of thoughts. Of what he would feel like if they kissed. Thoughts that she should not be having.

She should have stayed in London instead of running away for a month if she wanted a husband. Had she done so, even now, she may have met Lord Lyon and allowed him to court her?

But then you would never know if he married you for love or money.

True, she inwardly sighed. Pitying the woman he would marry in a small way.

He held out his hand, and Elena frowned, wondering what he was up to.

"Will you do me the honor and dance with me, Miss Smith?" he asked her.

Elena had slipped her hand into his before she thought to answer, eager to be near him, to touch him in any way she could. He pulled her against him, and heat kissed her cheeks. Her stomach fluttered, her heart beat loudly in her chest.

She wanted to be in his arms, to have him watch her as

he did right now as if she were everything he ever dreamed of, even if she were not. She could dream, could she not? That a man would choose a woman he believed to have nothing, and marry her anyway, even when he needed a wife that would save him from financial ruin.

He spun her into a waltz, and she laughed, forgetting everything that would keep them apart and instead throwing herself into the dance. He watched her, his eyes holding her captive, and she could not look away. He drew her in like a moth to a burning flame.

"You dance very well, Elena. How is it that a lady's companion is so very fluid on the dance floor?" he asked, his hand dipping lower on her back, his thumb running along her spine and making delectable goosebumps on her skin.

"I have been tutored in all dances, including the waltz. To be a proficient lady's companion, one must be able in all things."

"All things? Really? How intriguing that sounds," he teased, a mischievous quirk to his lips.

She wanted to kiss him. She wanted his lips on hers, no longer asking questions about her training as a companion, which was naught. She only wanted to feel him, to have him for herself.

To keep him here in Somerset for the month so there could be moments just like this one to enjoy. The thought of him leaving for London made her want to cast up her accounts. To hear of his marriage to someone else would surely kill her stone dead.

"Do not try to tease me into saying something that is inappropriate, my lord. I merely meant dancing, sewing, riding, and talking. All the things that you hired me to do while I'm here."

"You may call me Theo, Elena. I should have stated so yesterday when you offered me the use of your name, but no more titles between us. Not when we're alone."

"Then I suppose I should make use of using it here and now, for we cannot be alone like this ever again. It would not be wise or appropriate. As a companion, that is one rule that I am quite aware of." And as an unmarried princess, she was quite aware of it too.

Her sisters would skin her alive should they know she was dancing with an unmarried lord in a dilapidated ballroom in Somerset without a chaperone. And not just any dance, but the waltz.

"You have not made use of my name yet?"

Elena felt as though she stood on a precipice. That if she were to say his name aloud, everything would change. Their friendship, their ease and conversation, everything would alter.

But nor could she deny his request. It burned a way up her throat and out into the open, and there was no pulling it back when it was released. "You dance very well, too, Theo."

Somewhere within their conversation, they had stopped dancing, and they were merely holding each other in the middle of the room. His hand tightened on her back, stroking her through the muslin material of her gown. Never had the touch of a man, not in any previous dances she had taken part in, caused her to long for more of his embrace.

His eyes darkened, and she read the need, the struggle within his soul over what he wanted to do and what he should not attempt. She recognized the struggle, for she fought with it too.

Elena made the decision for him and reluctantly

stepped out of his hold. He did not need her muddling his mind any further than it already was. He was to London to find a wife. She was not ready to be one, not just any man's wife in any case. She wanted a love match, and as much as she respected and liked Lord Lyon, he did not love her.

You could fall in love with each other given the opportunity, a whispered voice taunted her.

Elena continued to inspect the room, forcing away the need for the man not a few feet from her. His lordship did not follow, and she was grateful, not certain she could deny him a second time should the opportunity arise.

"The dowager is probably free now, Miss Smith. You may go if you like, I shall see you at dinner this evening," he said, formal once again, the detached gentleman he ought to always be.

A stab of disappointment pierced her soul that he understood her rejection of him and conceded she would not be swooning in his arms any time soon.

"Of course, my lord. Thank you for the tour. I do hope one day to see the ballroom in its full brilliance."

He threw her a small smile, his face shuttered and guarded against any emotion. "Let us hope that you do, for I should like to see it as well."

With that, Elena left, making her way downstairs and back beside the dowager where she was safe from handsome lords. Gentlemen she was more than suitable to marry if only she was certain it was for affection and nothing else.

She could not abide a loveless marriage of convenience. That would never do.

CHAPTER 11

*T*heo lay in bed later that night, the moonlight and cooling breeze off the lake giving some relief to the hot and uncomfortable night. Not just because of the suffering hot days they were enduring, but because Miss Smith, Elena as he now knew her had put his mind into a spin and made his body a fiery tempest.

You want her.

His mother's companion.

He was a bastard even to contemplate such a liaison. She was an unmarried maid. Pure and sweet, delicate and capable, but poor. Had he money to burn, the courting of her in truth, of seeing if what he felt whenever he was around her ran deeper than friendship could have been a possibility. His mind and body had never been so stimulated as it was when in her presence. He looked for her everywhere about the estate and wanted to be near her whenever he could.

She was everything he had ever wanted in a wife. Kind and gentle, honest and forthright. No meek and mild miss, but not too boisterous to be unladylike. Miss Smith was simply perfect.

And as broke as you are, he reminded himself.

He thumped the bed with his fists, remembering the afternoon with her in the ballroom. He had wanted to kiss her. Had wanted to take her sweet lips and kiss them senselessly. He ran a hand over his jaw, aching for her still, and knowing he would never have her.

Someone else would marry her, a gentleman of her class.

He fisted his hands into the sheets, hating the idea of such a thing. He did not want her married at all. Not to anyone but him, at least.

You cannot have her.

He sat up as a sound outside his window caught his attention. He threw back the bedding and strode to the window, looking out onto the terrace below.

A woman in a night rail and gray shawl sat on the stone seats that ran along the terrace railings, a bright little light flickering in the darkness sporadically.

He frowned. Did Elena smoke? Curiosity got the better of him, and he strode from his room, determined to ask her of her habit, even if it was merely an excuse to spend more time with her.

It did not take him long to reach the terrace, and he came upon her just as she was butting the cheroot out on the dirt of a potted plant.

"Terrible habit, Miss Smith. I did not think ladies liked smoking cheroots," he teased her, smiling as her eyes widened at being caught smoking, and outdoors at this late hour.

Tonight at least, she wore a shawl over her night rail. Even so, he knew very well what she looked like under her gown. He had seen her in all her beautiful glory when her gown gaped in his study. Ogling her had been most inappropriate conduct he should not have partaken in, but he had not been able to help it. He had seen her and his mind refused to work after that fact. Each day since, and the more he came to know her, the more he wanted her with a hunger that scared him.

He could not dally with her. He could offer her nothing, but still, he found himself stepping out onto the terrace and seating himself beside her.

She smelled of sweet lavender, and he breathed deep, savoring everything he could about her person.

She chuckled, and her laugh made his lips twitch. "You weren't supposed ever to find out my vices, my lord. Can you pretend never to have found me and remain ignorant?" she asked him, meeting his gaze.

"I could never remain ignorant of you, Elena." And that was the crux of his problems. Now that she had stepped into his life, all others paled before her beauty, her sweet nature, and kind heart. Poor or not, he could see himself giving it all up, losing everything if only she would agree to be his.

But it is not only you. You have tenants, your mother, the staff, so many mouths depend on you keeping the estate and the lands you have left.

"You should not say such things, my lord," she stated, her voice hard, and shame ran through him.

She thought him a rogue, a gentleman who wanted to climb under her skirts and nothing more. And she was right. A part of him wanted her that way, but that was not the only way either. He simply did not have the means to give them both what they wanted, and he had King George to thank for that.

"I know I should not, but I find myself unable to stop thinking about you," he admitted, needing to tell her the truth no matter the consequences. He met her gaze, wanting to see her face and read her as much as he could. A small frown line sat between her brows, her mouth pursed into a thin line. "I can offer you nothing but friendship, Miss Smith. I would be lying if I told you that I do not want to kiss you. I want to kiss you until the sun comes up in the eastern sky, but I will not. Were I only rich enough, your rank and mine would not impede my courtship of you."

A small smile lifted her lips, and she reached out, clasping his cheek. He felt her touch, deep in his soul. How was he ever to let her go? How could he marry another when she drew him in so much more than anyone ever had in his life?

"I would like to be your friend, Theo. I do not have many I trust in my life, but I believe you may be one whom I can."

"Friendship will do very well, Elena." It would have to suffice as they were never able to be more than that. Not if he were to keep a roof over his head and everyone else's who relied on him.

She would forever be a regret, the woman in his life he let slip through his fingers, but there was little he could do about it. His current circumstances were unsurmountable without a rich bride, and as heart wrenching as the truth was, Miss Smith could never be the one to save them all.

*T*he dowager watched from an upstairs window as her son and Princess Elena spoke on the terrace below. She narrowed her eyes, wondering why they both looked so very pensive and grave. Sad, one could say as well, but why?

Had something happened between them that they did not like? Elena, in particular, appeared torn. The young lady really ought to own up to who she was, and she would speak to the princess about being truthful to her son tomorrow and see what she said.

How absurd for them both to leave the other behind simply because one needed a rich wife, and the other was pretending not to be wealthy, merely to hide from the *ton* for a month.

But to tell her son the truth would be breaking a promise she had made to Elena. She knew of the troubles the princesses had endured the last few years from their wicked uncle and then his thugs who tried to further dirty Atharia's water by causing trouble here in England.

Elena had been held captive at the castle in Atharia by her uncle, and the dowager could only imagine the horrors she endured there. It did not surprise her that the young woman had fled London looking for peace.

She kept behind the curtain, watching as the princess clasped her son's cheek. The dowager had an overwhelming urge to stamp her foot. They were simply perfect for each other and seemed to get along well enough too.

Not everyone had such ease with another, and they would be fools indeed to let what they so obviously felt for each other pass.

"Well," she huffed. "I will not allow you both to mess up a grand match, and my matchmaking skills will simply have to be improved," she mumbled to herself, determined to have her son married and to Elena before the Season was over.

CHAPTER 12

*E*lena carried the tray of broth and a hot cup of tea up to the dowager's room three days later after her ladyship had complained of a sore throat and a runny nose.

Since then, she had come down with a terrible cold and had gone so far as to ask her son to stay at the estate and not travel to London, even though his lordship had yet to agree to her request.

At this stage, Elena was starting to wonder if Lord Lyon would ever travel to London to find his rich bride. So many things had happened to keep him in the country, and she couldn't help but wonder why the poor gentleman was so unlucky.

Thankfully today, Elena had received mail from her friend Lady Villiers, Margaret, stating all was well at Kew Palace and that she had posted the first missive to Elena's sister in London. She had also enclosed a letter from Alessa that had arrived for her.

Apparently, there was nothing new and not a lot to report from town. Alessa seemed settled and had not mentioned traveling to Kew Palace to join the house party, even though she too had been invited. All good news and information that allowed Elena to breathe easier.

Had her sister decided to change her mind and travel to Kew, Elena would have had to leave, and she did not want to go anywhere. The thought of watching Lord Lyon depart the estate had left her more disillusioned than she ever thought to feel. In truth, she did not know his lordship very well, but her body seemed to ignore that fact and jump and shiver at the mere sight of him. She had never reacted to another gentleman so, and therefore she could not ignore her reactions to his lordship, could she?

The door to the dowager's bedroom was ajar, and Elena pushed it open, coming into the room to see Lord Lyon standing beside the bed, conversing with his mama.

"Oh, excuse me, my lady. Do you want me to leave and come back? I did not mean to intrude."

The dowager waved her into the room. "No, stay, Miss Smith. Theo was just explaining to me that now that I'm unwell, he will postpone his trip to London once again. I'm sure in a week or so, I shall be back to rights, and he can travel to town."

An absurd amount of hope thrummed through her veins at the knowledge that his lordship was not leaving them today. That he was staying made her want to smile, but she dare not. Instead, she schooled her features and reminded herself she had not traveled to Somerset to find a husband but to look after her mother's oldest friend and take some time away from society.

Of course, she had not expected the handsome, utterly seductive Lord Lyon, Theo, to remain here.

Her ladyship held up the newspaper she was reading, patting the bed for Elena to place the tray. "I was telling

Theo that the Queen of Atharia has arrived in London, and her sister, Princess Alessa, has announced a new women's shelter to be built near Bath. How lovely of them to care for more than their own people but those of their husband's motherland. I believe they both married Englishmen if I'm not mistaken."

"They did indeed," Elena said without thinking and closing her mouth with a snap before she said anything else. Like how much she adored her new brothers-in-law and the attention and love they doted on her elder sisters.

His lordship slumped onto a chair beside the bed, his face one of disdain. "More royalty who flaunt their wealth and think that they must save everyone. They live a life of luxury and little purpose while the poor, the children in the orphanages and shelters, live off scraps of food and clothing. They only help to increase their egos."

Elena frowned, hurt piercing her heart at his unkind words. Not to mention she knew very well what he spoke was untrue. "Princess Alessa's shelter for women is one of the best in England, if not Europe. The women who go there are fed and clothed and not walking about in rags, as you put it. I would suggest you correct your statement if you're going to pronounce untruths."

The dowager sipped her tea, her eyes wide and going back and forth between his lordship and herself. Elena narrowed her eyes on the marquess, wondering why his tone was so scathing toward a family he did not know. She knew he disliked his own sovereign, was his dislike of royalty extended to those from other countries as well?

"You approve of royalty lining their own pockets, living off the public purse, while their people suffer, starve and die of such malnutrition and neglect daily?" He shook his head, dismissing her. "I apologize if I offend you, Miss

Smith, but I cannot agree. I do not think any royal family, including the one here in England, should be the ruler of the country. They are out for what they can get, not caring about who they trample on their way to endless wealth. I cannot support such a dominion. Not now or ever."

His lordship stood and strode from the room. Elena stared after him, unsure of what had just occurred. He was so very angry, so very scathing of royal families and their charitable nature. Whatever would he think of her when he found out the truth of her life, who she was?

Would he hate her too?

"He does not mean what he says, my dear. He holds King George responsible for the loss of our land that made our circumstances more difficult. The lands, you see, supplied the majority of our income from harvests."

Elena slumped into a nearby chair, having not known that. "How is it that he thinks my sister's charitable nature is so very bad? She is only trying to help those without means to help themselves."

The marchioness reached out, taking her hand. "He does not mean it. He is angry and has held a grudge against the royal family since the day his father died. Do not concern yourself further regarding his thoughts on royalty. You are not here for my son, and he is not courting you, so you needn't worry about what he thinks."

Her ladyship's words were, of course, true. Even so, her thoughts on Lord Lyon had changed these past days to ones she did not understand herself. "He will not always know me as Miss Smith. He will think even less of me now, knowing that I am, in fact, a princess. He will think I came to Somerset to make a fool of him and trick him as to my true identity. If anything, it will make him dislike royalty even more." Elena swallowed the panic that rose inside her.

She could change his mind about her family and royalty, surely. He could not blame her for what happened between his father and the king.

"No, he will not," the duchess rebuked, but even Elena could see that her ladyship did not quite believe her own words. That she was concerned what Elena said was true. "You are not here for my son, and therefore he has no reason to consider you as a future bride. Or think that you tricked him merely to get closer to his person. You are here for me, which is true. Everything else that has occurred is merely a matter of circumstance."

Elena cringed, hating that his lordship thought so lowly of royal families, not just the English one, but hers too. A little unfair, in her opinion.

"I think I shall have rest now, my dear. Thank you for the tea, but would you mind calling in on me in an hour or so?"

"Of course," Elena said, standing and leaving the marchioness alone. She walked from the room, closing the door softly behind her. Elena looked up and down the passage, thinking of where Lord Lyon would be.

She needed to be anywhere but where he was. After their waltz last evening and then his opinions on royalty today, it was probably best that they keep apart. Keep to being friends and kept their distance.

That he would be remaining here for a few more days was a complication she had not thought to face, but she was a grown woman and capable of keeping him at bay and her emotions locked away. She was a princess, after all, and a master at hiding emotions when duty called.

．　．　．

*E*lena was able to avoid Lord Lyon for two days following his mother's sudden illness. He did not state if he noticed that she was not dining or breaking her fast in the morning with him. She assumed he understood she was with his mama, whom she had started to think was making a remarkable recovery and hardly looked ill at all.

Except when her son came to visit her, and then she seemed to wilt like a flower on a cool, frosty morning.

Today Elena was given a little time to explore the gardens. She had seen the river, but she wanted to visit the maze she had spied out the ballroom windows several days before.

She pulled a bonnet onto her head and exited the house through the terrace doors, starting for the overgrown maze. It was several feet higher than herself, and should she get lost within its paths, she would not be able to look over the top and work her way out of her predicament.

Even so, Elena entered the maze, confident that she would be able to make her way through the puzzle. She was a master of the mazes back at their estate in Atharia, and this one was a lot smaller, if not a lot more wild than she was used to.

For several minutes she wandered through the paths, turning here and there. There were small statues hidden in the foliage at several locations, an old shoe, and even a broken chair, which she had not thought to find. Did Lord Lyon even know what was in his maze?

The maze opened out into a clearing, and a large rectangular fishpond, dry and without waterlilies or fish, came into view. She wandered around it, able to picture easily how beautiful it once must have been. What a shame that it was all going to ruin and waste.

She turned, looking for where she entered and found the location, but after several minutes and returning each time to the pond, Elena started to think that this maze had beaten her at her expert skills after all.

No one knew where she was, a silly mistake that she had not thought to tell anyone before she left the house. She looked up at the estate, trying to see if anyone on the first floor may be watching her progress. No one stood at the windows. Even so, for a few minutes, she waved her arms about, trying to gain anyone's attention.

Elena slumped onto the side of the pond, listening out for any gardener or any servants who she may hear outside.

There was little she could do other than yelling out like a banshee but wait to be found. And with any luck, hopefully, that would be soon since it would grow dark in an hour or so, and she did not, under any circumstances, want to sleep outside. No matter how warm the night looked to be.

CHAPTER 13

Theo sent several maids to check the house's closed wings when Miss Smith failed to return to the house. He knew she had walked the gardens for a time, for a footman stated he had seen her earlier outside on the grounds.

Since then, no one had seen anything of her, not in the house nor grounds.

Theo left his concerned mother and raced back to the river. He feared finding her discarded clothing yet again beside the water's edge, but there was no sign Miss Smith had ever been there.

He skidded to a stop at the edge of the lake, thankful to find the area free of discarded clothing or anyone splashing about in the water. He turned, studying the grounds, thinking where she could have walked.

Had she strolled to the village? A possibility, but then at this late hour, surely she would have returned by now.

He started back to the house, walking the overgrown gardens before his attention snapped to the maze and the faint calling out from a feminine voice within it.

A grin lifted his lips. The maze was more difficult than people gave it credit, and certainly, it was even harder to navigate and remember the way in and out the more overgrown it became.

"Miss Smith," he called when he was close enough to hear that it was indeed Elena somewhere lost in the maze. "Where are you?"

He heard her mumble something before she called, "I'm at the pond at the maze's center. Please help me. I cannot seem to find my way out."

Theo made his way through the maze, making a few corrections himself as he headed toward the pond. It had been years since he had walked the paths, and the sight of the maze, and the poor condition it was in, left him disappointed. Everything about his home needed repair, money, so much more money than he had the ability to get his hands on.

He ought to have married already and had all of the house and grounds repaired. Had Miss Smith not entered his life, he would have left for London, no matter what issue arose at home, but with her being here, he'd used the excuse to remain and halt his plans. He should not have. He could not marry her, no matter how much he wished he could court her in earnest.

"I'm almost there, Miss Smith," he called, just before he came into the center of the maze to find her seated on the edge of the dry pond, a small leaf in her hand that she was rolling between her fingers.

She stood and came over to him. "I'm so glad you found me. I thought I might be stuck in here all night. I could not find my way out, and I kept getting turned about and ending up back here. I'm quite certain that your maze moves, my lord."

He chuckled and started back from where he came. "Come, I shall guide you to safety. It is not so very hard, not once you know all the tricks and secret turns."

She scoffed, but he felt her follow in his footsteps.

Theo made his way through the maze, the turns familiar, and he was certainly correct, so when he found himself back at the pond only minutes later, a look of amusement on Miss Smith's visage, he could not work out where he had gone wrong.

He turned in a circle, frowning. "That makes no sense. I know the maze as well as the back of my hand. I do not understand how we ended up back here." They attempted to exit several more times, and by the fifth attempt, Miss Smith's amusement had morphed into despair.

"We're going to die here, my lord. Trapped in a magical maze that does not allow anyone to leave once you enter its green cell walls."

He sat on the pond edge, just as Miss Smith had done earlier, and thought over the way out of this madness. "The maze is overgrown, and it must have changed the design so much so that I can no longer remember the way out."

She raised a skeptical brow. "And where does that leave us? We cannot sleep outside. Not together," she stressed, pinning him to the spot with her dark, earthy orbs.

Heat crept up his face, and he stood, striding for the maze exit. "Come, we shall not give up until I have saved us both."

He heard her sigh, but she followed him nonetheless, and so when they returned to the pond for the sixth time, Theo too was sure some trickery was at play.

Fate perhaps? his mind taunted

He rubbed a hand over his jaw, regarding Elena, and as

much as he wished her arrival here was fate, a savior to his desperate soul, it was not the case. Elena was as poor as he was, and they could not marry. So stuck together in a maze made little difference. Regardless if they were stuck overnight, he could not offer her his hand, even if he wanted to.

*E*lena made herself comfortable beside the pond and watched as dusk gave way to night. That she was stuck in a maze under a moonlit sky with one of the most handsome gentlemen she had ever met in her life was not ideal, given she was a maid and he was a man.

He stood at the edge of the maze, hands atop his hips and a fierce frown on his brow. She should not want to laugh, but the sight of his lordship not knowing the way out of his own garden feature was quite entertaining.

"No matter how much you stare at it, my lord, I do not think it'll change shape or magically open up and allow you to leave."

He sighed, facing her. "I admit, it has been some time since I'd come in here, but you would think I would know the way around my garden."

He came and sat beside her, leaning back against the pond just as she was. She supposed that seated as she was now meant her gown would look tattered and dirty when they were rescued.

"At least it is not complete darkness," his lordship said, staring up at the stars above. "We can see a little."

Elena studied him, drinking in his profile, his straight nose, and chiseled jaw. He glanced at her and caught her ogling him, and for the life of her, she could not look away. Nor did she want to.

The night was warm, fragrant of flowers and pine, and heat licked across her skin. The man at her side was a temptation she did not want to refuse, no matter how much she should.

She ought, of course. Lord Lyon was after a rich wife, a position she could fill, but she did not just want to be someone's means out of financial ruin. She wanted to marry for love, and nothing else would do. Even so, the next words out of her mouth would not be held back.

"Are you going to kiss me?" she asked him boldly, not certain where her gumption came from to ask such a thing, but the heat that flickered in his blue orbs told her she had read him correctly.

"Do you want me to?" he asked her, his tone serious, his deep, gravelly voice making her blood sing.

Her stomach clenched in delicious somersaults, and she nodded, hoping he could see her well enough to see her answer. "Do you not want to?" The words slipped from her, and there was no taking them back. She felt exposed and nervous, but also as if she stood on the edge of a precipice, about to jump into a wondrous new world.

He reached out and clasped her face in his hands, tipping up her chin and studying her. "I should not want to kiss you as much as I do, but you know that would be a lie. I want to kiss you, have wanted to kiss you from almost the first moment I laid eyes on you."

She shivered, licking her lips, as his words made her want him all the more. She reached out, clutching his shirt in her hands. "I would be lying if I said I have not thought about kissing you too."

With a slowness that threatened to make her expire from wanting, he dipped his head. She closed her eyes as his lips settled on the sensitive spot beneath her ear. She gasped, having not expected him to kiss her there first. She let out a breath, having not realized she was holding it.

This was madness. To kiss him made no sense, but she would not stop him. Oh no, she wanted him with an urgency that burned and ached in her blood, and there was no denying herself now his touch.

"You're so beautiful," he whispered against her ear. She swallowed, unable to comprehend that he had said such a wonderful thing. "Now that I've tasted you, I do not think I will ever be sated."

Elena slid her hands over his shoulders, feeling the corded muscles that flexed and moved as he kissed her. She wrapped her arms around his neck, wanting him closer.

His hair was soft and slid through her fingers like silk. She held on to him, wanting him with a madness she had not expected nor ever experienced before.

He kissed across her jaw, his hand holding her chin. Their eyes met, held, and time stood still. This was it. This was when she would have her first kiss.

In a moonlit garden with nothing but the stars as their witness. Their time here could not be more perfect. Excitement thrummed through her, and she bit her lip, waiting, hoping he would not delay any longer.

"I want you to kiss me," she said, pulling him closer, having enough of waiting. She had waited all her life for such a night, such a man to see her. Not just her name and wealth, her title and connections, her family, but *her*. Lord Lyon did not want the princess who sat beside him, but the woman she was.

No rank, no wealth, a lady he desired as much as she wanted him. It made the need for him all the more consuming.

"My lord?" a male voice called nearby, close enough that Elena knew they were in the maze somewhere.

"Damn it." His lordship cringed and pulled away, standing and moving away from her. "In here, Thomas," he called, just as the stable hand came into view, a small lantern in his hand.

"Ah, my lord, I thought that it might have been the maze that gained the upper hand on you both. If you wish to return to the house, I have marked a way out."

Elena stood and smoothed down her rumpled gown, taking the opportunity to turn from the men so she could gain her wits. After her near-kiss with Theo, her cheeks burned, and she had little doubt she would look flushed and needy.

"Very good, yes, lead the way, Thomas," his lordship said, turning and holding out his hand for Elena. She stepped before him, glad to have him at her back to give her time to compose her emotions. Thomas thankfully had no issues leading them out of their green prison.

A sweet jail, however, that would forever hold a special place in her heart.

Would Theo try to kiss her again at some other time and place while he was here?

She took a determined breath, stealing a glance over her shoulder, and found his heated, unwavering gaze on her person. She shivered, pushing down the need that rose within her. He would try again, she understood. It was only a matter of when.

CHAPTER 14

*T*he following morning Theo sat at the breakfast table, downing his third cup of coffee after his restless night. The woman sitting beside him all that his mind had conjured the moment he retired, an endless reel of memories of kissing her sweet, soft neck, of whispering against her ear, eliciting a shiver of awareness that had rocked his soul. She had smelled divine, and he would forever think of her whenever lavender floated in the air.

How could he ever keep her at a distance and stop himself from falling under her spell a second time? Of ignoring all his wants and desires and putting them second to his responsibilities.

He had gone to his mother once they had been rescued from the maze and explained what had occurred. He was pleased when she was not upset or cross with Miss Smith. He would have thought his mother would have been a little put out that her companion had disappeared most of the afternoon and evening, but she was not. If anything, she had looked charmed, and if he were suspicious, overly delighted at their predicament.

He frowned down at his half-eaten bacon and boiled egg, wondering at his mother's response. Was the dowager up to tricks he was not aware of? And if so, what did she hope to accomplish by pushing Miss Smith and himself together?

"The day is so lovely, not too hot, I think," his mama stated, sipping her tea and pulling him from his thoughts. "While I am not well enough yet to show Miss Smith myself, would you be a dear son and escort her to the local village? I know she wished to see it."

Theo met Elena's startled gaze, and he knew his mama had not mentioned the idea to her this morning. Did his mother think to send them off without a chaperone? It certainly sounded that way. Even so, he would like nothing more than to spend more time with her without the prying eyes of everyone under the estate's roof.

"We will have to walk, but it is not so far to be taxing. Are you up for it, Miss Smith?" he asked her. When she did not answer, he continued, "Unless you do not wish to, of course. The choice is yours." However, he hoped that she desired to go on the outing. A rejuvenating walk to the village would do them both good.

She placed her cup of tea on the table, nodding. "Of course, I would like that, thank you. When did you wish to leave, my lord?"

"After breakfast would suit best," Theo stated, not that it mattered what time they left, but the sooner he had her all to himself, the better. He ought not, but nor could he help himself. There was no denying him her company.

They finished their meal, and Miss Smith went upstairs to change into sturdier shoes and to grab her bonnet. His mama was nowhere to be found, having disappeared after quitting the breakfast room.

He stood in the foyer, pacing before the doors and front windows, his mind consumed with nothing but Elena. Well, that wasn't entirely true. He also could not help but think where he ought to be right at this moment.

In London, courting women of extreme fortune and nothing else. Certainly not his mother's impoverished companion.

As if his thoughts conjured her, Miss Smith started down the staircase, and he knew why he was not in London in that instant. As much as he required a wealthy bride, he did not want anyone else other than the woman who sauntered toward him. She was utterly beautiful in her light-pink morning gown and matching heavy pelisse. Her bonnet accentuated her high cheekbones and pretty eyes, and the breath in his lungs seized.

He would lose his estate, what small income they had left off the lands The Crown had not stolen from him yet, but he would have his title and Miss Smith as his bride. It would be enough.

Too many people rely on you, Lyon. You cannot be so selfish as to satisfy your own physical needs or those of your heart against your people.

It pained him to know what he ought to do versus what he wanted, but he had no choice. He had to marry well and discard the pull to his heart and mind that Miss Smith rallied within him.

Her lips quirked into a knowing smile as if she knew all his wayward, wicked thoughts, and he wished they were alone, lost in the maze where he could kiss her.

The timing of his stable hand had been unfortunate last evening, and he had dreamed of taking her lips, of having her in his arms just the way he wanted. Their walk into the village would not enable them to have any privacy, but he was a patient man and could wait. Hopefully, the opportunity arose before he left for London.

You cannot dally with her and then leave her behind, you rogue.

He sighed, bowing as she came to stand before him. "Are you ready, Miss Smith?" he asked her, fighting to remain formal and aloof.

She nodded and moved past him without a word. A footman opened the door, and they started down the stairs and up the long, gravel drive toward the village. "I must admit I'm quite looking forward to our outing, my lord. On my way to the estate the first day, I broke my journey at the inn and left early the following morning. It did not give me much opportunity to see much of the town."

Without thinking, he picked up her hand and placed it upon his arm. His need to touch her, to soothe his mind that she was real and his, for now, overriding the rules of respectability. She did not say anything about his behavior, but a douse of pleasure coursed through him when her fingers flexed on the coat, gripping him.

"The town is small, and I fear it may disappoint you. There is a small modiste whose husband is the village cobbler. There is the inn, of course, and a pastry shop. There is a park that houses a small fountain and a grassy area for children to play. But apart from those features, it is mostly housing for the local townsfolk. I do believe several of my tenant farmers have homes in the township too, preferring to live there than on the estate."

An issue he hoped to repair once he had the funds. They had to move out because he did not have the means to repair the roofs on their cottages.

"It sounds lovely. Should we visit the pastry shop and eat our lunch in the park? A spontaneous picnic sounds just the thing."

The excitement in her voice meant he could not deny her request. "I do not believe I have ever heard anyone be more enthusiastic for a picnic, Miss Smith."

She chuckled, smiling at the road before them. "I suppose I am. I have had very few, you see. But the one I had with the dowager marchioness several days ago was relaxing and enjoyable. I would welcome another."

"Your desire will come true then, Miss Smith. We shall picnic in the park and watch the world pass us by."

She glanced up at him quickly. "Please remember to call me, Elena, my lord. Miss Smith sounds so formal and cold. You have saved my life, and after last evening in the maze, well," she sighed contentedly. "I do not think formality is necessary. Do you not agree?"

Theo cleared his throat, having not expected her to bring up the subject of their near-kiss or speak so matter-of-fact about it. His body was still reeling from having her in his arms. He wanted her there again. Did she feel the same, or did gentlemen often throw themselves at her feet, and she was used to such things?

His stomach churned at the thought, disliking the idea she was often accosted by rakehell lords looking for easy skirts to lift. As a companion, such women were often used and discarded when their allure faded by men of his ilk.

"I should not have tried to kiss you last night, Elena," he admitted. He did not want her to think of him as such a man. He would court her, marry her should she agree, had he had the funds to do so. How he loathed King George and his greed that made such women as Elena no longer a possibility.

She waved his concerns away, staring ahead, a wistful smile upon her lips. "You were not the only one there, my lord. It was not entirely your fault if my memory serves me correctly."

"Theo, please," he asked her, wanting his title to be dispensed with too, at least when they were alone.

She grinned. "Very well, Theo," she said, warmth rushing through his veins at the sound of his name on her lips. "But as I was replying, you were not the only one there. I would have kissed you back, and gladly so."

Theo almost choked on his tongue. Never had a woman ever spoken so honestly and forthright before to him. But then again, never had he tried to kiss an unmarried maid. Certainly not one like Elena was turning out to be. So very different from anyone he had ever met before.

"Truly?" he asked her. "I do not want you to think that I'm some rogue who tries to kiss all of my mother's maids and companions, for I do not."

"I would not have allowed you to kiss me had I thought you that type of man," she stated, her tone brooking no argument.

They continued, coming to a crest of a small hill. The modest village came into view, little puffs of smoke snaking their way into the air from the few lit fires in the cottages.

"A kiss is harmless enough, Theo." She stopped, turning him to look at her. "I know you cannot marry me, and I do not want you to think that I shall allow you to sleep with me without the safeguard of marriage, but a kiss… Well, I may allow that to occur if we were to find ourselves alone together once again."

"Like now?" he asked her, stepping close.

She tipped up her face, watching him. Hell, she was pretty. Her dark locks brought out the color of her eyes. Her lashes were as long as any he'd ever seen. The thought of her kissing anyone other than himself was unfathomable.

"There is no harm in a kiss or two. We're both consenting adults, and I enjoy your company as I hope you enjoy mine. If we do happen to be alone, more alone than this," she said, looking about the dirt road they stood. "I would not refuse you."

Heat licked along his spine, and he wanted nothing more than to wrench her into his arms and kiss her until they both did not know where or who they were until they could not breathe from want of each other.

Instead, he held out his arm for her to take yet again. She wrapped her hand about his elbow, and he escorted her down the hill. "Let us hope that an opportunity does arise, Elena, before our time runs out, and I expire of want of you."

"Yes, let us hope it does," she answered him.

He couldn't agree more, and if he prayed hard enough, with any success, it would be sooner rather and later, and well before he left for London.

CHAPTER 15

*E*lena could not remember a happier day than the one she spent with Theo. They walked the small village for several hours, speaking to the locals and looking at the few shops the village was fortunate to have.

Elena had never been so free before. She had guards and courtiers following her in the past, maids and companions doting on every want and need. But here in Somerset, she had been able to remove herself from that glittering life and how liberating and wonderful it was.

Since the house party at Kew Palace was an event hosted by King George, even though he was not likely to arrive, she had not needed to take her guards or companions. As for her lady's maid who had helped her with her plan, she had paid her to travel to Kew and attend Lady Villiers and her maid, so she would not be left in London where her sister Alessa could find her and start asking questions.

Theo had taken her to the modiste and cobbler, not a lovelier couple Elena had ever beheld. They ate small iced cakes before the bakery window and watched children chase ducks about the park. Their sweet laughter made theirs break free, especially when one child was fortunate enough to catch one.

The people of the town treated Theo with respect and kindness, and she could see that it pained him not to be able to help when they requested it. He was the caretaker of them all, after all.

They had returned to the estate later that afternoon, her feet sore, her gown dusty from the walk, but never had she had a more enjoyable time. That her day was spent beside Theo had made it even more memorable, and she longed for it never to end.

Later that evening, she sat in the upstairs parlor the dowager particularly liked, sipping tea while the dowager knitted.

"What are you thinking about, my dear? You are very quiet with your thoughts just now," the dowager said, her fingers working quickly with the needles in her hands.

She wanted to tell the dowager everything. That she had started to adore her son and wanted him for herself. When he laughed, a warmth spread through her heart. When he watched her, his eyes dark with delicious intent, she could not deny him any more than she could deny herself.

But with each day she was a guest here at the estate, she also became more and more aware of his lordship's financial quandary.

The house itself, its run-down gardens, and peeling wallpaper were obvious enough. But having visited the town, seeing the tenant farmers who now had to find employment elsewhere told her his lordship was in a lot worse financial debacle than she first imagined.

Tenant farmers worked the land, lived in cottages on

the respective lord's property. They did not have to seek employment away.

"May I ask something, my lady? And please, do tell me to mind my own business if you do not wish to explain what is troubling me."

"Of course, I shall help you as much as I can. What is it that you wish to ask me, my dear?" The dowager settled her knitting needles in her lap.

Elena took a fortifying breath, needing to know the truth of the situation so she would know best how to proceed. "Lord Lyon is so very desperate to get to town, and I would like you to tell me if this is because he requires a wealthy bride?"

The dowager's mouth opened and closed several times before she sagged in her chair, her face a mask of pride, even after being asked such a difficult question.

"My son does need to marry well, and it is why he was to travel to London. We are at risk of losing the estate. Of course, Theo will keep his title, but the house will revert to The Crown if we cannot pay the taxes on the estate." Her ladyship sighed. "My husband was in a card game and lost a lot of our most valuable farming land to King George. When Theo inherited, he tried to make the land we did have in our name work to support the estate, but it was too dense with forest and wet for crops. The lady that my son marries will have to have a king's ransom to save us from relocating to London permanently. I have a townhouse there, you see, that I inherited from my grandmother."

A king's ransom. Or a princess's fortune...

Elena studied her hands, having known the truth of the dowager's words, but hearing them aloud made Theo's plight all the more real.

"He ought to travel to town and soon. The horse is

better, and the carriage is repaired, and you have recovered from your illness. He should leave as soon as tomorrow, for I would hate for you to lose this magnificent home over a foolish card game." And she would not marry a man unless he loved her for herself, not for who she was. Such a marriage would be the epitome of torture, and she could not stomach such a future.

The dowager smiled, picking up her knitting needles. "He will return to town soon and find a suitable lady. I know it was not the way he wanted to find his bride, but that is the way of the world. Not everything is fair and how we would like it."

The thought of Theo marrying a woman he did not love but required to save his estate also sent a chill down her spine. Such a marriage was abhorrent, and she could see why he was putting off traveling to London and choosing from the wealthy who desired a title and thought marrying a penniless lord was a good bargain.

His lordship's plight made it all the more important for her need to keep who she really was from Lord Lyon. Should their relationship progress further and she started to feel for his lordship more than friendship, then she needed to know that he loved her for herself, not for what she would bring to the marriage.

Oh, who was she fooling? She already had feelings for Theo that went deeper than mere friendship.

"I hope his lordship finds a woman who is not only wealthy, but one who captures his heart," she said, the statement only partially true. For she could not wish for him to leave and marry another, no matter how much she knew he needed to. She wanted him to stay here with her. To prove to her that a lord would marry a woman without a penny to her name. Even when that lord needed blunt more than anything in the world.

Only then would she trust that his love was true.

Her dream of such a thing was unlikely to come to fruition, but she could wish for the end all the same.

The dowager packed away her knitting before standing. "If you would excuse me for an hour to two, my dear, I feel in need of a little lie down before dinner."

Elena stood, going to help her. "Are you well, my lady? Would you like me to escort you to your room?" she asked, going to help her quickly.

The dowager shook her head, preferring to proceed out of the room without any assistance. "No need, my dear. My room is not far. I shall see you at dinner.

Elena watched her go and slumped back onto the settee. She had not seen Theo today, he had ridden out on the grounds early this morning on the back of his elderly horse, and her heart had hurt that he did not have a mount suitable for a marquess.

Theo deserved to be on the back of a thoroughbred, as strong and fast as those raced at Newmarket. He deserved everything in the world, and if he did choose her for his wife, loved her with all of his heart, then all his wishes and dreams would come true. He just needed to follow his heart instead of his head.

*T*heo took the stairs two at a time, striding with purpose toward the upstairs parlor. He came into the room and found the woman he was looking for. Thankfully alone.

Elena sat on the settee, a *Belle Assemblee* publication

open on her knee, casually studying the latest fashions available in London.

She was as pretty as a painting of sunshine and flowers. "Has my mother stepped out a moment?" he asked her, pulling her attention from the brochure.

"Oh," she stated, startled by his appearance. "Her ladyship has gone to lie down for an hour or two before dinner this evening."

"Very good," he said, closing the door. Before he could think better of his actions or remind himself why this was a bad idea, a very, very bad idea he should not attempt, he strode across the room, hoisted Elena from the settee, and kissed her.

Hard.

She gasped against his mouth, and he took the opportunity to tangle his tongue with hers. She was all softness and smelled as sweet as the hothouse in summer.

Should he have one. The estate had long given up such luxuries.

He expected Elena to pull away, to ask him what he was about. Instead, her fingers gripped the lapels of his coat and pulled him close, her mouth taking as well as giving in the spontaneous kiss.

Theo lost himself in the feel of her. She kissed him with abandonment. He thrust away all that stood between them. His lack of funds and hers too, and merely enjoyed having Elena in his arms. She made a soft, mewling sound that taunted his resolve to keep the interlude at a kiss.

He wanted to do so much more with her. He wanted to untie the pretty dress from her delectable body, slide it down her feminine curves, exposing her ample breasts and flaring hips. He wanted to kiss her everywhere, mark her as his in the only way he knew how, with adoration.

She stood on tiptoes, placing her height almost equal to his, and kissed him. Her passion made his head spin. How was it she could not be his? How could life be so cruel as to keep him from having her?

You could have her. It would mean the ultimate sacrifice.

Theo did not want to think about the problem now. He wanted only the woman in his arms and nothing else to distract him. He clasped her jaw, spiking his fingers into her hair and feeling it tumble about her shoulders.

He broke the kiss, her eyes glassy with need and passion stared back at him, wide and with a question within them.

It was enough to make him crumple to his knees.

He would bow down to this woman as poor as they both were if it meant that they would forever be just as they were now.

Together.

CHAPTER 16

*H*er kiss with Theo was like a dream. He was everything she wanted in a gentleman and hers for the taking. Tonight at least.

She kissed him back with all the pent-up and denied need that had thrummed through her these past days. She had wanted him like this for so long. To have him kiss her with such sweetness made her knees tremble and her heart race.

She could not get enough of him. How was she ever to watch him ride off in his carriage to London to marry another? She could not. She had to tell him the truth.

Tell him who she really was before it was too late and he found out by other means. A fact that would happen. It was only a matter of when.

Elena threw herself into the kiss, taking all that she could from the man making her want so much. Delicious things that she did not understand but desperately wanted to learn.

Did all kisses feel like this? Like she did not know how

she would ever return to earth, keep her feet on solid ground after the heights he threw her to?

His tongue tangled with hers, and she suckled his mouth. Her body was aflame. His hands slid over her back, down onto the globes of her bottom, wrenching her against his person.

His manhood jutted against her stomach, pooling heat at her core. She sought to satisfy herself against him and wanted to please them both, but she could not understand why.

She had never felt like this before. Her body did not feel like itself. It ached for his touch, more of his kisses, but not just on her lips, as wicked as they were there, but other places too.

Naughty, forbidden places upon her person she had never allowed another to know or see or touch.

Not until Theo.

She wanted him to know her. All of her.

"I want you, Elena, so very much. I ache for you. I've wanted you from the first moment I saw you step down from the carriage, so beautiful and confident."

She pulled back, sliding her hands over his shoulders, loving the look of dishevelment that had befallen him. He looked thoroughly kissed, his lips swollen and red from her touch.

Elena ran her finger over his bottom lip, soft and full. She wanted to kiss him again and again, knowing she would never be sated, not when it came to Theo.

"You did? How enlightening." She chuckled when he reluctantly stepped back but continued to hold her hand.

"You did not feel the same?" There was fear in his blue orbs, and her heart tumbled in her chest at his vulnerability.

She nodded, unable to lie to him about her feelings at least. "I did, of course, but then I'm a companion," she said, wondering when she would tell him the truth and if he would hate her for her deception. Now that she had included his mama in her lies made it doubly worse. But she wanted to hear that he cared for her, loved her, before knowing she was a princess and the answer to all his problems. Was that so very much to ask?

"I have no right in looking at you in a romantic light. I know I am not what you need." Even though she did see him as the man she wanted to marry. What a tangled mess she had weaved and needed to unfold before it was too late. She had fled to Somerset to leave the madness of London behind—including her life as a royal princess— only to find a madness of her heart here at Lyon Estate.

A madness she never wanted to end.

"Let us not speak of the difficulties that we face and merely enjoy our time together. I promise I shall not ask anything of you that will injure your reputation. No matter how much I may wish to."

With his words, he wrenched her back into his arms, kissing the underside of her ear, sliding his tongue along her neck, and eliciting a shiver of desire through her blood.

The man was impossible to deny. She did not care about propriety and what she ought to do and what not to do. For years she had stood behind her sisters, the third daughter of a king remembered more for her beauty than anything of substance. The man before her cared for her, a commoner, a woman without wealth or connections. That he did meant everything to her. It was as priceless as her jewels and estates combined.

No one had ever cared for her who did not know who she was already. Theo did not, which meant, with him, his affection was heartfelt and not brought on by what she could give him financially and socially.

It was an elixir more potent than pink champagne. And she adored pink champagne.

"I would like that very much. For now," she added. The next few days, she would bask in their newfound attachment. And then she would tell him the truth. He deserved to know she was no companion but the Princess of Atharia.

*J*ust as she wanted, Elena and Theo were inseparable over the next week. The dowager accompanied them on most of their excursions. They had revisited the maze, determined to find their way in and out within a few minutes this time, instead of hours like the previous attempt.

Theo's mama had watched from the lawn on a chaise brought out by one of the footmen and laughed as they called to each other within the green walls, working their way through.

Elena had made it to the dry pond first, determined to claim her prize.

"Lord Lyon, I do believe I'm the winner." She laughed, smiling as he walked slowly toward her, his dark, hungry gaze sending her mind to race.

"This time," he replied, stopping but a hand's length from her. "What do you wish for your prize to be?" he queried, not making another move toward her.

Elena closed the space between them, fisting the lapels of his coat within her hands. "You. I want you to kiss me again."

He growled, wrapping his arms around her back.

"Your wish is my command, Elena." Theo kissed her until she did not know how to stop, how to regain any sense of time or decorum.

His lips were soft, beckoned her like nothing she ever felt before. His strong, muscular arms pulling her against him, his manhood straining against her stomach made her knees weak, her body ache.

The kiss had been playful at first, filled with laughter and small nips, but it did not take long to change. Somewhere in their teasing, the kiss turned molten, hot and determined, demanding and consuming.

Elena could not get enough, and it was only when Theo's mama had called out to them, asking if they were lost, that she knew she was admittedly lost, not in the maze, but within her heart that was as tangled up with Theo as the vines about them.

"We shall be right out," Theo called, taking her hand and, this time, leading them out of the maze without any trouble.

The following day they had visited the folly for a second time, taking the opportunity to steal a kiss or two along the way when the trees and shrubbery hid them from the dowager who once again stayed at the bridge.

Their nights were filled with games of cards and parlor games with the dowager until she was too sleepy to remain and retired for the night. Elena, of course, retired too, but tonight Theo had a special treat for her, although she did not know what that plan entailed. She wore a morning dress of blue cotton along with a camisole, unsure what they were doing.

After midnight she snuck from her room and tiptoed downstairs, meeting Theo in the library. He held up a basket, a bottle of wine, and an assortment of sweetmeats and treats wrapped up in linen.

"A midnight picnic under the stars. The night is oppressively hot, and sleep will be almost impossible in any case."

Elena could see he was pleased with himself at his gift, and she was too. He was so very kind and charming. He deserved everything he ever wanted, and when he proved his love was true, she would give him the world if he only asked.

He just had to say what she needed to hear. Three little words. Words that she knew she had come to feel for him and would say back without a moment of hesitation.

"That sounds heavenly," she said, walking up to him and taking his hand, kissing him quickly since they were alone.

He hummed. "You are too tempting. Mayhap we ought to stay here instead?"

She chuckled, pulling him from the room and toward the front foyer and door. "No. Now that you have offered me a night under the stars, I want that, and no library will do."

They stole out of the house, running and laughing as they made their way out onto the unkempt lawns. Theo took her down toward the lake, a location hidden from view of the house.

He went over to a small tree, moving several branches to reveal a rug he had hidden there. Her lips quirked. "Did you sneak that out here today?" she asked him, looking forward to their time alone. As much as she adored his mama, it was so very lovely to be with Theo with no one else listening to their every word, watching their every gesture.

He shook out the rug, setting it on the side of the river, before holding out his hand and helping her sit. She kicked off her slippers and stockings, the cool air on her feet going some way in chilling her flesh on this hot evening.

Theo joined her, lying down, his arms settled behind his head, looking up at the stars. Elena joined him, having never been outside this late at night, taking in the heavens. She had, of course, stolen a look or two at balls and parties when she was taking the air on a terrace or gardens, but those occasions were nothing like the one she was now experiencing with Theo.

The night had no moonlight, and the stars shone so brightly and clearly. "Do you ever wonder if there is a world like ours somewhere out there? Do you think the many balls of light are planets or merely stars as we term them?" she asked him, curious for his answer.

"Hard to say," he replied. "But I like to imagine we're not the only ones. How marvelous that would be, do you not think?" He met her gaze, and Elena's stomach somersaulted. "That somewhere out in that great vastness, there is another couple, watching the heavens and thinking of other worlds too. I like to think there is."

His thought was a lovely idea to muse over. She turned, watching him, reveling in his handsome profile. Her heart pounded. How could she ever have thought to let him leave and marry some heiress in London? He deserved love, just as she did, and she wanted them to have it with each other.

She reached out, pulling his hand toward her, and kissed his palm. "Thank you for this gift, Theo. I do believe in all our adventures these past days; this has been my favorite."

Theo rolled to his side, watching her. His hand pushed a lock of hair from her face, slipping it behind her ear. "It is my favorite too," he answered before he closed the space between them and kissed her again.

And she was lost.

CHAPTER 17

*T*heo kissed Elena and lost his heart to the woman in his arms. Never had he felt such an overwhelming urge to protect, care, and love someone always, as he did with the woman beside him, kissing him back with an urgency and need to match his own.

She was a madness in his blood he could not cure. Nor did he wish to. He wanted her. All of her. He ought to tell her that he had fallen in love with her, but the words would not form.

He was a man, after all, and to pronounce such truth was never easy. Not to mention stating the truth meant he could never travel to London and marry a woman of wealth. He would lose his home, leave those who relied on him for employment without income. Everything he had fought to keep for so many years would be lost.

He desperately wanted to tell her the truth, but doing so would seal his fate. Seal all their fates to a life of moderation and little grandeur. No matter how desperate he was to make Miss Elena Smith his wife, forgo everything else he held dear, he could not form the words.

But he would have her tonight. He would love her in the only way he could.

She pushed him onto his back, and he chuckled, having not expected her to take command. He adored that she did and took what she wanted, no matter that she was the fairer sex. Elena was no meek and mild miss.

"I adore being here with you," she whispered against his lips. He clasped her face, kissing her hard. His hand followed the line of her spine, making her squirm before he kneaded her ass.

She had perfect globes, a lovely handful. She moaned and the sound proceeded directly to his cock. He ached with a delicious need that rode his every touch and kiss he bestowed upon her.

She slid her leg over his waist, placing herself directly upon his rigid manhood. The urge to hoist up her dress, to spread her legs and sheathe himself into her warmth hungered through him.

Instead, he lay patient, reveled in her movements as she settled atop him, undulating against his cock, teasing them both.

She placed her core directly over his manhood. He moaned, breaking the kiss and steeling himself to behave. "You drive me to distraction, Elena."

She sat back, pulling him up by the ties on his shirt. Her features were no longer teasing or amused but solemn, her dark eyes a pool of need.

"You drive me to distraction, Theo," she said, repeating his words. "I want you too. Please let me have this one night in your arms," she asked him.

She would have more than just this one night. He would make certain of it. He took her lips in a searing kiss, the madness within him changing everything. Elena ripped his shirt from his breeches, tossing it to the side somewhere on the river bank.

Theo worked the buttons on her camisole before going to work at the back of her gown, thankful when it gaped enough that she could shuffle out of it. With her dressed now in only her shift and corset, he made short work of the strings hiding her delectable self from him, the corset landing somewhere on the grass. They would worry about finding it later.

He rolled her onto her back, settling between her thighs. She wrapped her legs around his hips, biting her lip as she worked herself against him. He could feel the dampness of her sex. Even so, he reached between them, teased her mons, flicking her extended nubbin until she moaned.

He loved the feel of her, hot and wet. His mouth watered, wanting to taste her sweet flesh.

"Oh Theo," she gasped, her fingers scoring the skin on his shoulders. "Please, do not tease me so," she pleaded.

He wanted to do so much more than fuck her with his hand. He wanted to lick between her moist lips. Flick her nubbin and have her clasp his head with her legs as she came against his mouth.

He wanted her in every way a man could have a woman. Spend the rest of their days and nights locked in each other's arms.

Not able to wait for a second longer, he ripped at his front falls, his rigid cock spilling into his hand. Determination sparkled in her eyes as he set himself at her core.

"Are you sure, Elena?" he asked her, needing to hear that she agreed to what they were about to do. For after it was done, there was no turning back. No stopping what would befall them both. Marriage, a life. Even if that life was a frugal one.

She nodded, spiking her hands into his hair and pulling him down for a kiss. The sweetness of it took his breath away. "I'm certain, Theo. I want you."

She pushed up against him to prove that point, and he lost the small amount of control he still commanded. He thrust into her, sheathing himself into her tight, welcoming heat.

She gasped and stilled, and he paused, giving her a moment to get used to him. "It will not hurt for long, my darling. I promise to make this night one you shall forever remember."

Her wide eyes soon lost the small amount of fear they held, and after a moment, she relaxed in his arms, her legs hooking about his ass. She shifted, seeking him to move with her. He did not need any further urging. Theo rocked into her, giving her what she wanted. What they both did.

The sensation was nothing like he had experienced. The woman in his arms captured his heart and mind, and having her, making her his in this way, knowing he would be the one and only man to lay claim to her sweet self, humbled and stimulated him beyond measure.

They fell into a steady rhythm. Elena kissed him, sought him to go deeper, faster, and he gave her all that she wanted. He took his pleasure, sought hers, and would not disappoint, no matter how much he wanted to spend.

He pulled down one side of her shift, exposing a pink, pebbled nipple, and took it into his mouth, kissing her sweet peak, suckling her, and eliciting a gasp of awareness.

He did it again and again, teasing her other breast and giving her what she wanted. All the while, he thrust into her heat, her legs tight bounds against his back.

"Theo," she gasped, biting her lip and throwing her

head back against the picnic rug. "Oh, Theo. Yes," she moaned, her hand's tight bonds on his arms.

Theo thanked God when the first spasms of her release pulled about his cock. He was not sure how much longer he could hold out. He thrust harder, faster into her, and she clung to him, rocking against him, lifting up and seeking pleasure.

And then she shattered. The contractions, the spasms about his cock pulled his release forward. He came hard in her, emptying his seed into her welcoming flesh.

She moaned his name, reaching up to kiss him as the last of her spasms subsided about his manhood. He continued to rock into her, milking every last drop of ecstasy he could.

He slumped to the side, his breathing ragged, before pulling her into the crook of his arm, kissing the top of her head. "That is not what I planned when I sought your company out here this evening, Elena. But I cannot regret what has happened. You have made me the happiest of men."

She grinned across at him, her cheeks pinkened from their exertions. Her breast still gaped from her shift and teased his senses. He looked away from the tempting sight and planned when and how he would marry her. Explain to his mama that they would lose everything because he could not live without the woman in his arms—the woman at his side.

Miss Elena Smith, a companion who had captured a lord's heart and soul.

"You have made me the happiest of women. I adore you," she admitted to him, kissing him lightly on his chest.

He held her closer still. Tomorrow, he vowed he would

propose. She would be named the future Marchioness of Lyon, and nothing and no one would change that fact.

CHAPTER 18

The following morning Elena woke and broke her fast in her room. She bathed and dressed and was ready for the day before nine. She glanced at the clock in her room, knowing the marchioness would not be up for several more hours.

After her wicked night in Theo's arms, she had expected to sleep in late too, but she was too excited to lay abed. Not unless she was lying abed with her lover. Her future husband if she could get him to admit his feelings before he knew the truth of her life.

She had thought he would say something last evening, and in fact, several times she had thought he was about to admit to what he felt for her, but then it never happened.

Even so, she did not doubt what he felt for her would soon be admitted, but she needed to know in truth. She had to hear it for herself, and then she would know their marriage would be a love match, made to last until the day she passed, just as her sisters' unions were.

She swiped up her light shawl that sat over one of the settees, starting out of the room and down the passage—

determined to seek out Theo, who ought to be in the library by now, since he usually did estate work before noon.

Her steps faltered, and dread rolled down her spine at the sound of her sister Alessa's stern voice, demanding Lord Lyon tell her where her sister was located.

She bit her lip, wondering if it were too late to run away yet again so that she did not have to face what she was about to walk into.

She could hear Theo debating Alessa's words, explaining that she must be mistaken for no royalty stayed at Lyon Estate. That it was only his mother and her companion other than the few staff he kept on.

This could not be happening. How had Alessa found out? She calculated in her mind how long she had been in Somerset and figured she had at least ten days left before the house party at Kew Palace came to an end.

With nothing left for it and never a coward, she continued down to the foyer. Making the landing, she noted the door to the library was open, giving her a view of the room.

It was worse than she first thought. Not only was Alessa in the room, Rowan towered behind his wife like a mono-lith of deadly strength, and Holly and Drew were in atten-dance as well. She blinked, fighting nausea that rose in her throat when all at once, in synchronized horror, they turned to view who had intruded on their conversation.

Alessa slumped in relief, coming toward her and pulling her into a quick embrace. Elena's gaze met Theo's over her sister's shoulder, and she saw the confusion in his blue orbs.

She hated that she had placed him at such a disadvan-tage. He had deserved to know the truth so much earlier than now. And he certainly did not deserve to find out about her family in this way. It should have come from her.

After he had told her he loved her.

Elena was sure that he did, but he had not said nor offered for her hand. If he were to offer now, he offered to a princess. A woman rich enough to save his estate, his name in marriage. She loathed the idea of such a proposal, cold and required, not heartfelt as she had hoped. He would feel compelled even more so now that he knew who she was. A gentleman who had debauched a lady always did right by her and offered her his hand.

Would he?

"What are you doing in Somerset, Elena?" her sister Holly demanded, her voice regal and hard. Elena cringed, knowing her sister the queen was in a temper from the actions that had placed her here in Somerset.

Alessa walked her into the library and closed the door on the few staff who had stopped in the foyer, suspecting a dignified visitor they were yet to name.

Elena dipped into a curtsy before Holly, before bussing her cheek in welcome, trying to soften her sister's mood in any way she could. "I needed to remove myself from London, and an opportunity came to travel to Somerset and look after mother's dearest friend from the year she came out here in England. I saw no harm in that."

"Only that you were not supposed to be here in Somerset. We believed you to be safe and secure at Kew Palace attending King George's house party. He notified me that his cousin from Atharia had not arrived after a fortnight of the party commencing."

Damn the king for ratting her out to her sisters. He never attended his own house parties, preferring to keep to

Windsor. How like her luck to end. To be found out during the individual moment she tried to escape.

"Are you acting as a companion, Elena?" Alessa asked, looking between herself and Lord Lyon. "As his lordship has stated? Are you a servant here?"

The abhorrence of such a thing was easy to hear in her sister's tone. Elena knew she could not lie, not anymore, even if those lies would hurt the one person she never intended to injure at all. She was not supposed to have fallen for Theo, but she had. And now he would be angry, and would no doubt feel betrayed.

She had lied to him. Worse still, she was royal, a privilege that had caused his family so much pain.

"I applied for the position of companion for the Dowager Marchioness of Lyon, but only because I knew that she was friends with our mama and his lordship needed someone to care for her while he was in London."

Rowan scoffed behind his wife's shoulders. "His lordship seems quite settled here in Somerset, Elena. We have not seen Lord Lyon in town."

"That is because misfortunes have occurred to keep him here, but he always intended to leave," she said, defending his activities.

Holly narrowed her eyes, studying her, and Elena fought not to blush, not to react to her elder sister's inspection. What was she trying to find out about her? Did she suspect something?

God, she was thankful her sister, the queen, could not read minds.

"Elena or Miss Smith," Holly stated, meeting Theo's schooled gaze. "Is better known as Princess Elena of Atharia. Sister to a queen and royal subject of Atharia.

She is no companion and certainly should not be looking after anyone but her duty to The Crown and her country."

Theo's lip curled in scorn, and a little part of her died that he loathed her true self so much. How would they ever repair the damage her lying had caused?

He stood, legs apart and hands clasped behind his back. "I did not know Princess Elena as anyone but Miss Smith. I was unaware of the ruse that she has undertaken to remain here in Somerset. I can only offer you my apology and best wishes to her for the remaining season."

Elena felt her mouth gape. Was she so easy to dismiss? Would he not even fight for her? What was Theo about?

Alessa came to her side, taking her hand. "Elena, you look distressed. Has something happened, my dear?"

Holly gasped, coming to stand on her other side and pinning Theo with a loathsome glare. "Is there something going on between the two of you? For there better not be. I know of Lord Lyon's predicament and his need for a rich bride. It is why you were to travel to London, is it not?"

Theo glared at Holly, and Elena stilled. Never had she seen him appear so enraged. "Spoken like a true royal," he spat. "So long as you are well-to-do, nothing else matters, does it not?" He chuckled, but the sound held no amusement. "I do believe other than Lord Balhannah in this room, Sir Oakley came into your family with far less than I."

Rowan shrugged, throwing a placating glance at his wife. "He does have a point, my dear," he stated.

"That may be the case," Holly declared. "But when it comes to our younger sister, the rules change. She has not been out in the world as much as Alessa and myself, and I will not have her used. Not by you or anyone in need of funds."

"Holly, stop, please. This is a conversation I need to have with his lordship alone. As much as I love you and Alessa, this is none of your business." Elena wasn't sure where the gumption came from to speak so to her sisters, but it was time she defended herself and battled her own problems. If there was any chance for her and Theo, they needed to be alone and not have anyone else putting in their opinions.

"Very well," Alessa agreed, starting for the door. "We shall remove ourselves and let you speak alone. But not for long, mind you, and the door is to remain partially open to preserve your respectability."

There was little chance of preserving that. Not after last night. The memory of her time with Theo made her shiver with renewed awareness.

Elena watched as Holly and Alessa, along with their husbands, strode into the foyer, leaving her with Theo.

She walked up to the desk, holding it for support. "I'm sorry, Theo. I wanted to tell you sooner, but then I could never find the words. I wanted..." She could not form the words to tell him the truth, and he studied her, knowing she wanted to say more.

"Wanted what, Elena? What did you want?" he demanded, his voice hard.

She sighed, supposing there ought to be no more false-hoods. Not anymore. "I needed to hear that you loved me before you knew who I really was. Home in Atharia and here in England, people only ever say what they think I want to hear. They are only friends with me so they can say they have a princess as an ally. Husband hunting has been difficult as Princess Elena. But as Miss Smith, well, it has been a refreshing change. Nor," she continued, "did I set out for your estate expecting to meet you and share what we have, for I did not. But now that is what I want. I want a husband who loves me for me, and I will not settle until I gain that dream."

He slumped into the chair behind him as if his legs would no longer hold the burden of her words she thrust upon his shoulders. "You're a princess," he stated, his voice devoid of emotion. "No matter what you hope for, that changes everything."

She frowned, sitting down herself. "What I said to you was the truth, Theo. I had to leave London. For my own sanity, I could not stay there a day longer. My good friend Lady Villiers agreed to help me. She is also attending the house party at Kew Palace, and I charged her to send letters to my sisters to make them think I was there."

"And yet you were not. You were here. Under my roof and caring for my mother. She will be so disappointed to find out that you lied to her."

Elena froze, and the concern on her face must have registered with deadly grace. Theo leaned forward, pinning her with his dark gaze. "She knows, doesn't she?" He swore and stood, pacing behind his desk. "My mother knows you're Princess Elena of Atharia?" he scoffed, shaking his head. Elena wanted to go to him, but she knew the truth would be difficult for him, but she had wanted to know that his feelings for her were true, not born out of necessity for her wealth.

"She does. The first day I arrived, she recognized me as my mother's daughter. We are alike in appearance, you see. I made your mother swear not to say a word. I was desperate to stay and did not want to go to Kew Palace and pretend to be happy there."

"So you pretended to be a servant here?"

Shame washed through her that she had lied, but there

was no taking back her actions. "You were not meant to stay. I did not think it would trouble you, even if you later found out because you would be happily married and returned with your new bride. I would be back in London and no harm done to anyone."

"But harm was done, was it not, Your Highness?"

"Please do not call me that, Theo. I'm Elena to you."

He shook his head, denying her words. "No, you are not. Nor were you ever."

CHAPTER 19

*T*heo could not believe what he was hearing. How had she pretended to be someone she was not? How had she allowed him to care for a woman who did not exist?

What was he to do now? To marry her now would make him look the biggest fiend in London. But to not? To lose the woman he loved was also unbearable to contemplate.

She lied to you. She's royalty.

"I am Elena to you, just as you are Theo to me. That does not need to change. Nothing else needs to factor into our life."

"Of course it changes everything, for I have not done the one thing you want," he spat, running a hand through his hair. "Do you not see? You're royal. Cousin to King George. The very man who has done nothing but make my life hell." He shook his head. "I did not declare myself to you when you were Miss Smith. To do so now is not going to win me your trust. You will think, just as your sisters will, that I'm a fortune hunter. And I am. By my own words, I needed a rich wife. That has not changed."

Elena paled, and he reined in his ire. Damn it all to hell. How had Elena turned out to be the very being who encompassed all that he'd set out to loathe his entire life? Royalty? He could not believe it, nor did he want to.

Fate could be fickle. He knew that well enough, but cruel too? That was a new development, at least for him. Even so, he wanted to go to her. Wrap her in his arms and promise he loved her before he knew of her life. But would she believe him? He did not think so. There would always be a snippet of concern that he had married her for her money.

"His Majesty is a very distant cousin, and we are not cut from the same cloth, Theo. It is wrong of you to think of me in the same way. I'm not English, and my character is very different. I would never have cheated your father."

"You did not tell me the truth," he stated. He knew why she had not said a word. Hell, in truth, he would not have said a word either had he been in her situation.

"The more we grew to know each other, the more I understood the reasons why you shunned royalty. I feared your reaction to the truth of my life, and as time went on, it became harder and harder to declare myself. Not to mention I was desperate for a man to fall in love with me. Me," she pointed at her chest, hammering home her point, "plain and common Elena. Not the diamond-encrusted princess I usually am."

"A blind excuse," he spat at her, leaning on his desk and forcing himself to breathe. "You do not trust my character enough to believe what I say. If I were to tell you that I loved you now, would you believe those words? I do not think you would. That is the truth of our situation, is it not?"

For a moment, she did not say a word before she lifted her regal chin, commanding respect. "Was I wrong in waiting to see how you felt about me? Even after last night," she stated, lowering her voice, "you did not declare your love for me or ask for my hand even after all that we did. How can I not think but a little if you did so now it is because of my fortune?"

"And that is the crux of your problem."

"Not completely," she continued. "You will be marrying into royalty should I accept your hand of marriage. Had you offered it, of course. An institution you despise. Marrying you, I fear that in time your disdain for English royalty would spill over toward the Atharia lineage. After what King George did to your family, I would not blame you if it did, but it would break my heart to be the cause of your pain."

Dread loaded in his gut, hearing all the reasons why they should and could not be together. If only he had not told Elena he needed to marry well to save his estate, her declaration of truth would not factor. But his pride, his love for the woman before him, stopped him from asking now. He could not form the words, no matter how much he wanted her for herself and bedamn the inheritance.

But none of that mattered now, for she would never believe him should he ask. He could see it in her face, the hurt, the fear that she would only be married for what she would bring to the union, not because of who she was as a woman.

The image of his father hanging from the rafters in the attic floated through his mind. He could not marry royalty.

The very thought of doing so made him want to cast up his accounts. His father had been there for several days, and Theo had found him, the sight he could not remove from his mind, no matter how much he wished to.

King George had done that. Royalty and their selfish, commanding habits had killed his father. A future together would never work.

"I do not know what I believe right now. There is much to think about, and it is unlikely my sisters will allow me to stay and muddle through it all with you," she said, tears welling in her dark orbs. His heart broke at the sight of it.

"For what it is worth, Theo, I am sorry. I never meant to cause trouble or hurt anyone with my plan. I simply wanted to disappear."

He could understand her wanting to do such a thing. Hell, being a royal, British or otherwise, would not be easy. But he could not stomach her lies or what they made him if he married her now. Not with her at least. He could not marry a woman he loved, who did not trust him. His marriage to an heiress would be a marriage of convenience, a mutual trade. He could offer Elena nothing, for she had everything already.

"You will return to London with your sisters?" he asked her as the silence between them stretched.

"Today, I should imagine. There is much to think about." She picked at one of her fingernails as she held her hands in her lap. "Will you tell me why you dislike King George so very much? It cannot be solely because of the land you lost to His Majesty."

Theo saw no reason not to tell her. To explain, as much as he hated reliving everything about that time. "My father hanged himself in this very house. A year after he was

131

cheated out of the land in a card game with King George. When the lands were gone and the next harvest season was complete, the full effect of our loss came to fruition. My father could not live with the shame and took his life. King George, selfish, greedy royal bastard, killed my father and did not even send condolences. I have little time for anyone of his ilk."

"And that now includes me?" she asked him, her eyes shining with unshed tears. He pushed down the urge to go to her, to say he did not see her as the same, but what did it matter now? She saw him as nothing but a fortune hunter, his declaration of love too late to make any difference to their life.

"You should leave, Elena," he said, sitting at his desk and pulling his ledgers close, needing to go over the numbers before he left for London. However, this time he would go, carriage wheel broken, sick mother, or lame horse or not. He would leave.

"Well," she said to him, her tone chill. "I wish you all the best with your trip."

"I wish you well too, in finding a man who loves you for you and not your title," he called after her when she started for the door, back rigid and head held high.

Theo watched her leave, hating that she did not look back. He could see her sisters in the foyer and his mother too. Elena hugged his mother and kissed her cheek before being escorted out the door and into the waiting carriage.

He saw the gold royal emblem of Atharia on the door as it moved past his window and then down the drive. Lord Balhannah and Sir Oakley cantering after the carriage on their mounts.

His mother barged into his office without knocking, coming up to his desk and standing over him.

He did not bother to look up. His anger not wholly directed at Elena but his mother too. At King George. Every bastard who courted Elena for false reasons and made her disbelieve everyone's words. Including his. "You can leave, thank you. I have work to do."

"No, you do not. The only work you need to do is to get those carriage horses hitched and go after that young woman. You care for her, do you not? How can you watch her leave without any remorse?"

Oh, he had remorse, but he also had pride, and he would not have his affections toward her be tarnished or determined to be brought out of his need for blunt. To chase her down now and throw himself at her silk slippers would prove to her he had only wanted her for her money and nothing more.

To her, at least.

There was little he could do now to prove that was not the case.

"You knew she was a princess and played her game against your own son. How could you do that to me? How could you not tell me the truth?"

His mother surprisingly looked bashful, and so she should after what she had done. "She begged me, Theo. And her mama was a good friend. I could not throw her out when she was so desperate to stay."

He watched his mother, thinking over the past weeks. "You planned everything, did you not? The broken wheel the day after she arrived. The horse's lameness, your illness." All of it was making sense now. "Did you think to make me fall in love with a companion, knowing our predicament while knowing all along that I could not? That to marry Miss Smith would mean we would lose everything. But you did not know her as Miss Smith, did you, Mama? You knew her as a wealthy princess. The savior to all our troubles. How could you plot such a thing?"

His mother held up her hand, gesturing to the library about them. "What is the meaning of all of this if there is no love, Theo? I lived a marriage without affection, and it was like hell on earth. I would not wish such a future on anyone, and certainly not my son. I saw the opportunity for you to marry a woman whom you love, despite not knowing who she *really* was. And she loves you because you love her for herself and not her title."

He shook his head, dismissing the notion. He would not allow his mother to make sense of this situation or explain her actions away. "You know what royalty has done to this family. How could you allow me to court a woman who is a princess?"

"Please," his mother spat, walking to the windows and looking out over the grounds. "Your father knew what he was doing in that card game, Theo, and anyone who believes otherwise is a fool."

He stood, eating up the distance between them. "You allowed me to believe King George cheated my father. Are you saying that is untrue?"

"I did not think it would ever matter that you knew the truth, but your father was a compulsive gambler. He would have wagered you had he had the chance. You are fortunate that it was only the parcel of land of this estate that he lost. We could have been living in my townhouse in London for years had he wagered the entire estate."

Theo felt the room spin. This could not be true. Their monarch had tricked his father. He had died because of the treatment from The Crown. They had pushed his father to leave them all behind. Their greed had driven his family to the brink of financial ruin.

"What King George did that night with your father was agreed upon by both men, and your father was happy to wager part of the estate, so long as he had his cards in hand. What your father and King George partook in has nothing to do with Elena. It does not matter if she is royalty or lied. She does not deserve to be thrust to the curb because you cannot look past your own pride or what you believed to be the truth."

Theo ran a hand over his jaw, needing time to process all of this. "I shall be leaving for London tomorrow."

His mother clapped, smiling. "Wonderful. I do hope Elena accepts your proposal."

He strode to the door, wrenching it open. "Not to propose to Elena but to find a rich wife to save this crumbling pile of bricks. There is nothing to say between the princess and me. She wants a marriage of love and affection, and no matter whether I feel that way for her or not, she would not believe me now. I did not tell her how I felt before knowing who she was, and so all your plotting and planning has failed, Mother."

His mother was quiet a moment before she said, "You're a fine gentleman, loving and true. I'm certain that you will come up with something to change her mind. Do not return home unless you have her in hand. I will never forgive you if you bugger this up, Theo."

He strode from the room, needing to be alone. There was nothing he could do. For he may be a fine, loving, and true man, but Elena was wary and suspicious of people's motives. She was lost to him, but he could still save his estate, and that had to be his focus now. And Miss Smith,

Princess Elena or whomever she called herself, would have to be a pleasant memory of his past so that he could capture his future.

The future of his estate and all those who relied upon him deserved no less. His heart be damned.

CHAPTER 20

"What were you thinking running off to Somerset as you did? What possessed you to act so rashly? If there is a problem, Elena, you must come to me so I may help you," Holly said, her voice stern, but Elena could see in her eyes she was genuinely worried about what she had done and did not want it happening again.

"I could not stay, and that's the truth of it. I dislike society, the balls, and parties. Do you not think it is all so false and calculating? Every night reminded me of our plotting, vengeful uncle, and I had to get away. And so when the opportunity arose, I took it."

"Your friend Lady Villiers was displeased to have to tell us the truth, but when we arrived at Kew Palace to see you, and you were not there, we knew she would be aware of your whereabouts," Alessa said, watching her husband on his horse beside the carriage. "And we were not wrong but terribly worried until we saw you again."

"I hope you were not unkind to Margaret. She did not

want to do what I asked her to perform, and none of this was her idea. I merely dragged her into my plan," Elena admitted, hoping her sister did not think badly of Margaret, for she did not have an unkind bone in her body.

"We were not unkind, but Margaret did as we bade when I reminded her that should anything untoward happen to my sister the princess, I would blame her, no matter whose idea to hide at Lord Lyon's estate it was."

Alessa turned to face her. "Talking of untoward happenings, you seemed quite attached to Lord Lyon. Has anything happened between the two of you that Holly and I need to know?"

Elena swallowed, her stomach fluttering at the thought of Theo. Could it have been only hours ago she had lain in his arms in exquisite bliss? She closed her eyes and took a fortifying breath. She had never been able to keep secrets from her sisters, not ones as important as her connection with Theo, and she could not start now.

"I'm in love with Lord Lyon, and I did believe him to be in love with me," she answered truthfully, wishing that things had turned out differently between her and Theo.

"Had he stated as much?" Holly asked, whatever reaction she was having to Elena's words schooled behind a queen's composed visage.

"He never said the words, no, and I was hoping that he would before he knew who I was, but then you two arrived and stole that possibility from him, and me for that matter."

Alessa gasped, clutching at her throat. "Excuse me, but we did not know you had been fluttering your eyelashes at his lordship. And he should have stated he loved you if, in fact, he did. All we can hope is that your reputation will not be affected, and you can return to society without any harm done."

Elena doubted that could be the case. How could she walk back into society and not long for the man she had left in Somerset? If only he had told her he loved her before knowing she was an heiress, a princess. Then she would know that his love was true.

Perhaps all men made such passionate, sweet love to women, and she was no one particularly special. For all she knew, he may have up and left for London had her sisters not arrived and married another under her nose. Now she would never know what could have happened or if her opinion of him was correct or utterly wrong. At this point, she did not know what to believe.

He may have also stayed and declared everlasting love to you...

"If he loves you, Elena, he will travel to London and chase your skirts about town, fighting for your hand and trust. He will soon get over the shock of knowing you are royal and remember that you touched his heart. Nothing will keep him from your side, not even his hatred for King George."

Hope sparked within her at her sister's words. Holly had always been wise, and Elena hoped what she said did indeed come true. "Do you think so?" But then, was she ready to believe his love even if offered after knowing who she was and what that meant for his family? She would be a financial savior to him, but she wanted to be so much more than that.

"Of course I think so," Holly declared, settling back in the squabs. "And if he does not, then he is a fool not worth your hand."

Alessa sighed, again staring at her husband, who was also staring at his wife. Elena fought not to roll her eyes at the couple, who appeared more in love now than when they first married.

"But if anything has happened between you that progressed further than words or maybe even a kiss, then that changes things, Elena," Alessa declared, her pitch light, but her words marked with immovable steel.

"That is true," Holly added. "You must marry him if your relationship with Lord Lyon has progressed so far as to put you at risk of carrying his child, no matter if he dislikes royalty and you dislike people using you for what you can give them."

Elena's cheeks burned, and she fought not to blurt out the truth. Her sisters stared at her with unnerving calculation. As if they were trying to read her mind. She waved their concerns away, not willing to tell them everything. Not yet, at least. "Nothing of the kind occurred. Please do not ask me again," she lied, some things best kept to herself and not others. They had only been together one night. She would not know for weeks if she were with child or not. As her friend Margaret had stated to her, it was unlikely that a woman ever fell *enceinte* the first time she was intimate with a man.

"I'm happy to hear it," Holly said, a small smile quirking her lips. "We will be back in London tomorrow morning, and then we shall reenter society and hope Lord Lyon realizes his heart is no longer his own and returns to town."

"It does not change the fact that Elena will not know if he loves her for herself or her money. How will we know he loves our sister and not merely the fact she could save him from losing his estate?"

A question Elena had been asking herself all morning.

"I do not know how he will prove his worth, but he did not seem a stupid kind of man. I'm certain he will make amends and come to his senses. Only a fool would allow Elena, princess or companion, to slip through his fingers."

"Valid point, sister," Alessa agreed. "Let us hope he is not one of those."

Elena chewed her bottom lip, hoping her sisters were right, but a little piece of dread bubbled away inside of her, and she could not help but think her life was about to get a lot more complicated before it became anything else.

*J*t was three weeks before Elena heard the first whispers of Lord Lyon's escapades in London since his arrival the day after her own. The whispers confirming Elena's worst fears. Lord Lyon, Theo as she still affectionately thought him, was indeed, stupid.

Or he was acting as one of the most foolish men she had ever known. Tonight would be her first time out in society since her rendezvous to Somerset, but Alessa had called earlier that afternoon and regaled all that she had witnessed of Lord Lyon's escapades of the night before at the Johnson's ball.

Elena thought that since he had never seen her as anything but his mama's companion, that tonight he would see her for who she truly was. On the outside, at least. She knew he disliked royalty, vehemently so, but would he continue to carry that hatred over to her? She had not been the one to have gambled with his father.

While she felt for Theo, and the loss of a parent he suffered, to hold a grudge against her was absurd.

One could say the same to you about disbelieving his feelings when you know he loves you.

Elena stepped into the ballroom of Lord and Lady Hargrove. Her sister the queen announced to those in attendance before her, and Alessa followed. She entered behind each of them, raising her chin as they made their way into the room. There was little fooling anyone that they were the highest part of society which one could climb. The deep bows and curtsies as they passed, the warm welcomes and sighs of wonder followed them at every event.

Of all the people who were there, Elena only wanted to see one gentleman here this evening. To see for herself if he would fight for her or discard her as she feared he was doing. They positioned themselves near a partially open window that gifted them with a cooling breeze in the stifling hot weather London, and England too, were suffering through.

Thankfully her friend Lady Villiers joined them and pulled Elena away. She went willingly, only too happy to catch up with her friend instead of standing by her sisters to be ogled like some ancient, priceless relic.

Margaret dipped into a curtsy before bussing her cheeks. "Your Highness, how lovely to see you again. I missed you at the house party, and I must apologize for what has occurred. I know that your sisters fetched you from Somerset as fast as their carriage would carry them to you."

Elena fought not to roll her eyes, knowing that if they had not arrived, she may have known by now if Theo did, in fact, love her for herself and not for what she could give him. She would know if his love for her overrode his long-held hatred of the crown.

She sighed. "Yes, they did as you can see, and while I'm happy to see them again and you as well, their arrival at Lord Lyon's estate brought with it more trouble than my being there ever had."

"Do tell?" Margaret asked, intrigued.

Elena told her of her happenings there. Of her friendship at first with his lordship and then the mutual attraction that blossomed. She dare not tell anyone that she had given herself to him, but even now, she could not help but wish their parting had been different. That had he merely said those three little words, they may already be married and happily so.

"He is here, do you know?" Margaret asked, taking two glasses of wine from a passing footman and handing one to Elena.

Butterflies took flight in her stomach at the thought of seeing him again. It had been three weeks since they had parted. It felt like a lifetime, and she was yet to see what he was doing about London that was the current on dit. If Alessa was right and he was here seeking a rich wife, notably not her, she would know he had acted falsely in Somerset. Or was too pigheaded to admit when he was wrong.

"I did not know if he had arrived as yet," she answered, fighting the urge to glance about the room.

Margaret scoffed. "I'm surprised you did not feel the heat of his gaze upon your person when you entered the room. His gaze did not move from you, and I do believe his mouth was gaping quite unfashionably."

Elena swallowed her nerves, wondering if he were watching her now. "I will need to speak to him at some point, I suppose. But if he ignores me, then I shall know the truth, that he is like so many men of our acquaintance." But the bitter pill that Theo was just another rogue, financially bankrupt, and looking for salvation was hard to swallow. She so wanted him to be different. To prove he was who she needed him to be. That he may not be was too heartbreaking for words.

CHAPTER 21

Three weeks he had lived without Elena, and it was the longest three weeks of his life. Having arrived in London a day after the princess, he had thrown himself into society, attending every ball and party he was invited to. He rode each morning in the park and at the fashionable hour, doing the pretty by those he needed to concentrate on, winning over their mamas and paying endless compliments.

The whole time he felt like an old, creepy man trying to rob a baby from a cradle. None of the young, rich debutantes took his fancy. None of them were interesting or could hold a conversation above those of horses or fashion. The three weeks in town were the worst of his life, and his mother's words kept repeating like a drum in his mind.

Do not return home unless you have her in hand. I will never forgive you if you bugger this up, Theo.

He knew what the gossips were saying about him in London. That he was after a rich wife in need of a title. Any family on the up and up who needed the aristocracy to get there ought to apply. That Lord Lyon would do perfectly well.

Several nights he had drunk away his woes at his club, regretting his choice, not just imbibing, but also his intention to cast Elena to the wind. To allow his hatred of royalty, the grudge he held toward them to spill over into his feelings for Elena. To allow her to find love not brought on by the love of her wealth.

He was sick of wishing he had told her he loved her earlier. There was no changing that fact now. But worse was he knew she had heard the rumors about him in London. There wasn't a person present who had not. That he was seeking a rich bride and had not once attempted to reach out and speak to her.

He hated to think what she thought of him. She undoubtedly thought him the false rogue who slept with unmarried companions and then discarded them when they were not whom he believed. He needed to fix the error of his ways. Throw away his pigheadedness and fight for what he wanted.

Elena...

Theo remembered to breathe at the sight of her as she arrived for the Hargrove Ball. He had never seen anyone of such beauty, of regal elegance. She was utter perfection, and his chest hurt at the sight of what he may have lost.

Elena looked perfectly at ease in this society, as a pillar of what others fought to achieve. She was achingly beautiful, and memories of their one night beside the river swam through his mind.

Her laughter and sweet smile. Her intoxicating kisses that he wanted with a need that frightened him.

She had lied, yes. She was royal, a position he had loathed for so long he did not know any different. Even now, he found it hard to believe his mother's words regarding his father that his parent had been a compulsive gambler, willing to risk anything so long as he was dealt a hand.

Granted, Theo had been a young man, barely sixteen when his father had died. What his mother stated could be true, for how much had he really known his father? Very little when he thought about it. His father was rarely home and did nothing with him when he was back on holiday from Eton.

His mother would not lie, and she knew her husband better than Theo ever would know his father. He had determined, therefore, that what she stated had to be true.

But then, where did that leave him and Elena?

For the hundredth time, he cursed himself a fool for not telling her how much he cared for her, loved her. How he wished he had said so beside the river. How he wished her sisters had not arrived and he could have said it in the library.

Now she would never believe him, and he knew to marry her, to declare himself now would make him look a liar. His pride told him to let her go, but his heart could not.

It wanted her and no one else.

He sipped his whisky, remembering a saying his mother had mentioned to him before he left for London. That pride always came before the fall.

He caught sight of Elena through the crowd, wanting her with a need that would not abate.

"Lord Lyon, may I introduce myself correctly? I'm Sir Rowan Oakley, Princess Alessa's husband." Sir Oakley held out his hand, and Theo shook it, surprised the gentleman had sought him out. Especially after their short and to-the-point meeting three weeks ago in Somerset.

"Sir Oakley, good to see you again," he lied, not wanting a confrontation, certainly not at the Hargrove ball. He had enough of arguments these past weeks, most of them with himself.

Sir Oakley sipped his whisky, coming to watch the *ton* at his side. "I come in peace, I should add, my lord. I know what it is to love a woman so far above one's station to think one is not worthy. The other week at your estate, I felt as though the events caught you unaware. Have you thought over Princess Elena's possible involvement in your life? Do you care for her enough to love and protect her always?"

Theo adjusted his cravat, uncertain whether he could trust Sir Oakley with his answers. He was related to Elena, after all. His loyalty was to her.

"I do not know what Her Highness has explained to you, but I require a wealthy bride to restore my family's fortunes. Princess Elena wants a marriage of love and affection like her sisters. Even if I offered such a future, she would not accept me. I had a chance to ask for her hand before finding out the truth of her life, and I did not. She would not believe me."

"Have you asked her?" Sir Oakley raised a skeptical brow. "I have found that the truth, when spoken from an honest place, is believed. You should ask her and see. She may surprise you." Sir Oakley downed the last of his whisky. "But should you continue to court women as you have been these past weeks, continue to be the talk of the *ton*, you will lose Elena forever. It is something to consider when following a course that is not the one you should travel." Sir Oakley slapped him on the shoulder and left, walking back to where Princess Alessa and Elena stood with Lady Villiers.

What would he say to Elena? Throw himself at her feet and beg forgiveness for being such a dolt in Somerset? He rubbed a hand over his jaw, knowing he had to change his ways—tonight and not tomorrow. Tomorrow may be too late.

His heart stopped at the sight of Elena being led out onto the ballroom floor by Lord Legar.

The sight of her clasped on another man's arm left a sour taste in his mouth. There was little chance he could stand by and watch her marry.

She had not looked at him the entire night, and he wanted her to look at him now. To see what her being in another man's hold was doing to him—ripping his heart out and trampling it with her silk, diamond-encrusted slippers.

That she was royal no longer factored in his decision. He knew she was dubious of him, but he did love her, and she would come to believe him in time. He would spoil her, dote on and love her with everything he had. She would later think herself a fool for thinking he did not.

Not that he truly believed her to be foolish. She was scared of making the wrong choice of having a loveless marriage that would last a lifetime. But he knew better, knew very well she had no reason to be fearful of him. They may have started not as truthful with each other as they ought, but they would not end that way.

They would not end at all.

CHAPTER 22

*E*lena's feet ached as she sat down to supper later that evening. Her sister the queen had left earlier, needing to attend another event. Alessa and her husband, Sir Oakley, were the only two who remained, acting as chaperones.

Elena sat with Alessa and her friend Margaret, not the least hungry as her stomach churned at the sight of Theo seated with a group of gentlemen and several ladies at a nearby table. All of whom seemed quite rapt in their conversation with the marquess.

Was he looking at the pretty young debutantes as potential future brides? She fought to mask her emotions, but she could feel herself welling up at the notion of him marrying someone whom was not her.

"The man has been watching you all evening, Elena. The longing alone in his eyes should be enough to tell you that he's utterly in love with you, even if he has not stated so."

Alessa's words pulled Elena from her muddled thoughts and whether she should flee the ball and return home never to venture out again. Or even better than that, return to Atharia and join a nunnery.

"He never told me and has not sought me out here in London. What am I supposed to surmise from that? I shall tell you what I suppose, that he does not care for me at all. Certainly does not love me as I had hoped." As much as she loved him, even though she too may not have said the words, it was only right that a gentleman declare it first.

Her brother-in-law, Rowan, ate the last of his crab. "As a man and one who has spoken to Lord Lyon this very night, I will tell you that I think you're wrong in believing his feelings for you are superficial. When I joined him, his attention was fixed on you, not anyone else. No matter what you may have heard, I think it's a ploy. I think he is trying to persuade himself that his pride is more important than his heart. You wounded the poor fellow, you see, Elena."

"How so?" Both Elena and Alessa said in unison.

Rowan grinned, leaning across the table to ensure privacy. "You cut off his bullocks in a sense. He does not want to marry for money but needs to keep his estate and everyone who relies on him safe. But he fell in love with a companion, a woman playing a game, and he feels cheated. The woman he fell in love with does not exist, not in the way he thought she did. He wants to marry the princess she truly is, but he would be known as a fortune hunter, a term spoken aloud already in some ballrooms."

Elena supposed that could be true. She fought not to roll her eyes at her own thoughts. Of course it was true—all of it.

"You want a love match, but do not trust yourself to know when you've found one. I know you wanted him to say those words to you before he found out who you are, but you would be a simpleton indeed if you threw him aside because you do not believe what your heart is telling you as truth and trusted your mind instead."

Alessa nodded, silent as she took in her husband's reading of the situation. "I do believe Rowan is correct, Elena. What does your heart tell you?" she asked her.

Elena glanced to where Theo sat and caught him watching her. Her heart jumped, her blood rushed, and she knew without a doubt that he loved her, missed her as much as she missed him.

A small smile lifted on his lips, and she could not look away. How she wanted to wrap herself up in his arms. Be with him and ignore all the tattle regarding their marriage should it occur.

Some would say he married her for her fortune, and she would let them think that. But she knew the truth. He would marry her because he loved both the commoner Miss Smith and the royal Princess Elena.

"It's telling me," she said aloud, hoping Theo could read lips, "that I love him too."

Rowan smirked, and Alessa reached across the table and patted her hand. "Maybe there is another who needs to hear those words, Elena?"

"I did hear them," Theo said, walking toward her to stand at the side of the table. He stared down at her, and hope burst through her like a rush of pleasure. "I heard them as clear as if they were spoken without any distance separating us."

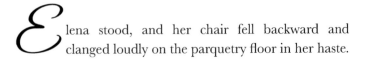

lena stood, and her chair fell backward and clanged loudly on the parquetry floor in her haste.

Her heart beat fast, and she hoped that she did not succumb to the vapors and crumble at Theo's feet.

He stood at her side, a towering man of sweetness and handsomeness combined. How could she have thought for one moment that he did not care for her? Love her? It shone from his eyes and was clear to see by anyone taking any heed of them.

"I love you too," he said aloud. Loud enough for everyone in the supper room of the Hargrove ball to hear. Gasps sounded about them, wistful sighs from ladies wishing for similar outcomes from their prospective suitors.

Elena could not shift the slow smile that formed on her lips.

Theo reached out and took her hand, kissing her gloved fingers. "My declaration is long overdue, I know. I put my pride first and told myself daily that I was keeping away from you, for you, that this is what you wanted. But I realized that I could not do that. Not if I wish to be happy and have a fulfilled life. Having you as my wife will be an honor, and so I'm asking you, Miss Smith, Princess Elena, whoever and whatever you are, to marry me."

Elena bit her lip, having thought that she would never hear those words. Not after the many weeks they had been apart, and the last time they spoke being less than ideal. "I'm royal, Lord Lyon. Are you certain you wish to marry a princess?"

He pulled her closer, nodding. "I was a fool to judge you along with the English monarch. My father was not wholly innocent in his dealings with King George. My continual hatred of The Crown is over and I will never mention his gambling and the outcome of that night again."

The music started up again, and Alessa stood with the

help of her husband. "I think our attendance at the ball has come to an end. Let us return to my townhouse where you may discuss matters further, but without the *ton* looking on."

Elena glanced about the room, noting the many pairs of eyes and rapt attention of guests they were holding. Theo held out his arm, and Elena wrapped her hand about it, reveling in the feel of having him so close once again. How she had missed him. The three weeks without him, their conversations, picnics, days basking in the sun at his estate, very much missed.

"That would be preferable," Lord Lyon stated, leading her out of the room, and if their evening went as planned, leading them into a future.

Together.

CHAPTER 23

When they returned to Princess Alessa and Sir Oakley's home, they retired to the drawing room, enjoying a refreshing cup of tea together for a half-hour, idle chitchat filling the awkward void that Theo and Elena had a lot to discuss, before the princess and her husband, a burly, bruiser-looking kind of man, bid them goodnight and left them to their own devices.

Not that Theo was complaining of being alone with Elena. He had longed for such an opportunity, had wished that he had seen her at the events he attended over the past three weeks, but then also grateful he had not.

She did not need to have the memory of what a total ass he had acted before the *ton* in trying to persuade himself of things he wanted that he did not.

Elena sat beside him on the settee and turned to face him once they were alone. She was everything a princess ought to be. The diamond tiara sat across the bridge of her head. Ornamental roses sparkled in her dark hair. He could see the question in her eyes, wondering if he was truthful with his words back at the ball.

Theo reached out, taking her hand in his and holding it against his heart. "I was a fool who allowed a past that had nothing to do with you or who you are to affect my decision. I came to London seeking a rich wife, to prove to you that I would not marry you for your money, and yet, I cannot marry anyone. I cannot stomach being with anyone other than the woman before me. Even if that woman is wealthy, a princess and heiress who would save my broke self. It is you whom I fell in love with, and so I am asking you to trust what I say is true, that I've been a fool and will never hurt you again. That I will love, honor, and adore you for the rest of our days if you will only give me a second chance."

Elena did not say a word for a moment, and he remembered to breathe, holding on to the fact she was here with him. That she had mouthed the words *love* across a supper room.

Those words had been for him. No one else. She would forgive him, and they would marry. Nothing else would do.

"I will forgive you, Theo, if you forgive me. I know you thought me common, Miss Smith, but I'm still the same person inside. I did not mean to lie and make you look like a fool. I'm sorry I did not trust in what I felt for you, what I knew you felt for me." She shuffled closer, and Theo took the opportunity to wrap his arms around her waist. "I find it hard to trust people's true motives. I should never have believed that just because you were not given the time to state what I thought you felt meant it was no longer true. That you did not love me."

"I love you so very much," he declared, wanting her to hear it again and again if only to dispel any lingering doubt.

She reached out, clasping his jaw. "I love you too. We

have both been so very foolish, but no more. Tonight we start anew, and in three days, you will marry me, Lord Lyon. I will hear of nothing else."

He grinned, kissing her quickly, needing to taste her before he expired. The kiss lingered, and he deepened the embrace, wanting her with renewed vigor. "I think with our connections, we can arrange a marriage in three days, and I cannot return home until you're my wife in any case."

Elena frowned up at him, a question in her dark orbs. "Whyever not?" she asked.

He chuckled, taking her lips yet again. "Mother told me not to return home until I had you as my wife. So glad that I will. I am particularly fond of my estate."

She laughed, and after weeks of living behind a drizzly, dark cloud, the sun burst into his world and made everything well again. "I'm fond of it too, and I have plans. As the new Marchioness of Lyon, it is only right that I make our home our own."

How could he have been so fortunate? How could he have the fortuitous event that gave him both a woman he loved more than life itself, along with a fortune? He had not thought he would have both. His marriage to her would save them all. He owed her so much, more than he could ever repay.

But he would repay her by adoring her always.

"You have saved me, you know. In more ways than you shall ever realize."

She smiled up at him, tears in her eyes. "Make love to me, Theo. I have missed you so very much. I do not think I can stand another moment of not being with you."

Theo kissed her hard, needing no further prompting.

What his future bride wanted, he granted. He would never disappoint her again.

*E*lena gasped as Theo took her lips in a searing kiss. He came over her on the settee, pushing her into the plush, velvety cushions beneath her back. The feel of his weight eliciting a shiver of expectation. How she had missed him, them, this, since the last time they were together.

The kiss was demanding, wild and wicked and set her heart to race. Unlike their night at the lake where they savored every touch, every kiss, tonight was different.

Theo settled between her legs, reaching beneath her skirt and teasing her wet, aching flesh.

"Oh yes, touch me," she begged, needing more. So much more. She undulated against his hand, seeking release, wanting what he could give to her.

He moaned, kneeling between her legs and pooling her skirts at her waist. She wore drawers, and he untied the little strings holding them at her waist, sliding them down and off her legs. The night air kissed her skin, but she was not cold. Not with the thought of what they were about to do.

Other than her evening gown and silk stockings, she was bare to him. His eyes darkened with heat and need, and before she knew what he was about, he was kissing the inside of her thigh, working his way up her leg.

Elena bit her lip and thought that she might die of embarrassment or longing at any moment, she wasn't sure which, before he kissed her where she ached most and she was lost.

She gasped, having never felt anything so exquisite

before. He lathed, suckled, and teased until she thought she might go insane with want.

She clutched at his hair, holding him against her as he worked her to a frenzy. "What is this madness?" she asked, never wanting it to stop.

"Just me, loving you in the way I have wanted to for so long."

His muffled, deep voice soothed and excited her. She undulated against his tongue, his wicked mouth, seeking the glorious release she had with him before.

And then he was above her, kissing her hard, his large, engorged cock pushing into her welcoming heat. Elena wrapped her legs about his waist, pulling him to her with haste. Fully sated, she sighed, knowing this was what she wanted. To be full and inflamed by his love.

"I love you so much, Elena. I have missed you," he breathed against her lips before kissing her with a passion that left her breathless.

How she loved him too. More than she ever thought to love anyone in her life. He was everything to her, the reason she would give up her life in Atharia and remain in England. The man who would be the father of her children. The first and last man she would ever kiss and give herself to.

Theo thrust into her with frantic and wicked strokes that sent her wits spiraling. Elena worked with him, moving and taking all that he gave. The need within her built, her body standing on a knife's edge, wanting to jump into the endless chasm of pleasure.

And then she fell.

Elena moaned his name through his kiss, never wanting the satisfaction to end. He loved her until the last of her tremors eased, and then he let go, spending within her, her name a chant on his lips.

One she would never tire of hearing.

He chuckled, coming to lay at her side, pulling her against him on the settee. Their breathing ragged, their brows damp from exertion. Elena smiled into his chest, kissing him there as the thought that in only a few days, she would be the new Marchioness of Lyon.

A wife. And if she were fortunate, a mother soon enough.

As if he read her mind, he tipped up her chin, catching her eye. "Three days, Princess, and we will be married. I hope you can pull a wedding together on such short notice," he said, a teasing light in his blue orbs. "Because I cannot wait a moment longer," he declared.

She smirked, knowing she would have no trouble whatsoever. "It will be no issue, I promise, and then you'll be mine, Lord Lyon. Mine to love and do with as I please. Mine forever," she said, hardly able to wait to see him again, and he had not even left yet.

He kissed the tip of her nose. "Mine forever too," he declared, and her heart was full. Fuller than she ever thought it could be.

EPILOGUE

hey were married three days later as planned and were only a few miles from Lyon Estate. They had agreed to surprise his mother with their marriage and arrival and hoped she would not be too upset she had not attended the wedding. Elena did have a little news tucked away in her heart that she was sure would please the dowager and repair any disappointment she may have had in missing the nuptials.

How she longed to be back at the estate, to start repairs and see that it was restored to its former glory. To give her sweet, new husband everything he deserved after going without for so long.

Under the seat opposite them sat a box with a piece of parchment she intended to give Theo, but she needed to ensure they were almost home before she did so.

She knew he would hardly be able to contain his excitement, and he would want to celebrate, and one could not celebrate in a carriage, not very well at least even though they had found other things to do in the equipage on their way to Somerset.

They rolled through the small village not far from the estate, and Elena knew it was time she gave him her wedding gift.

She kneeled on the floor, opening the seat and lifting out the parchment from the box within. Theo threw her a curious look, clearly wondering what she was about.

She handed the rolled parchment to him, watching as he unrolled it and read the contents. Elena sat beside him, a frown on his brow as he studied the deeds to land.

He glanced up at her, his eyes wide with shock. "You bought the land back from The Crown? How did you manage to do such a thing?"

She shrugged, grinning. "King George is a distant cousin as you know, and no one ever likes to have disagreements in families. I asked, offered a reasonable sum, and he accepted. Lyon Estate is back to its original holding size, and it is my gift to you for loving me just as I am, not for who I am."

He shook his head, for a moment lost for words. "I do not know what to say, Elena. Thank you does not seem enough."

She reached out, stroking his jaw, loving every facet of him and his character. His good, honest heart, his sweetness and wickedness combined. "That is not all. I have another gift for you too."

He beamed, picking her up and depositing her on his lap. "What else does my clever wife have for me?" he asked, teasing her with a kiss.

She moaned when his hand squeezed her bottom, pulling her against his hardened manhood, jutting against his breeches.

"I'm going to have a baby," she declared, hoping he would be pleased. When he did not say anything, his face paling, fear fluttered in her stomach. "I know we've only been married a day. And we have not known each other all that long compared to other couples, but I think this is wonderful news. I love the idea of us having a child, possibly an heir, to take on Lyon Estate. Do say you are happy, for I do not think I could bear to hear you are not. Theo I—" He pinned her lips closed with his fingers, stalling her words.

"You're rattling on again, my dear, and there is no need. My wits are back, you may have shocked me a moment, but that is all."

She smiled, biting her lip in anticipation. "You are happy?" she asked again, needing to hear that he was.

"Elena, I could not be more so. A child. Our child. You have made me the most fortunate of men."

He kissed her then, took her lips in a searing capture that left her breathless and the footman waiting when the carriage rolled to a halt before the estate.

Theo helped Elena step down from the carriage and, bending, swooped her into his arms, carrying her through the front door of the estate. She laughed, having not expected him to do what he did.

"Welcome home, my love," he said to her, not attempting to set her down once they stepped into the foyer.

She clutched him about the neck, playing with the hair at his nape. Her heart could not be fuller for the man who held her, would evermore love and protect her. "Welcome to *our* home, my love," she amended, kissing him again and knowing she would always adore him so. Her husband and friend.

Forever her marquess as she would be forever his princess.

Dear Reader,

Thank you for taking the time to read *Forever My Princess*! I hope you enjoyed the third and final book in my, The Royal House of Atharia series.

I'm so thankful for my readers support. If you're able, I would appreciate an honest review of *Forever My Princess*. As they say, feed an author, leave a review!

Don't forget to check out my new series, available February 2022, The Wayward Woodvilles! If you love Dukes and scandal, you'll love this new series coming soon!

Alternatively, you can keep in contact with me by visiting my website or following me online. You can contact me at www.tamaragill.com or email me at tamaragillauthor@gmail.com.

Tamara Gill

A DUKE OF A TIME

THE WAYWARD WOODVILLES, BOOK 1

Available February 2022!
Pre-order your copy today!

ABOUT THE AUTHOR

Tamara is an Australian author who grew up in an old mining town in country South Australia, where her love of history was founded. So much so, she made her darling husband travel to the UK for their honeymoon, where she dragged him from one historical monument and castle to another.

A mother of three, her two little gentlemen in the making, a future lady (she hopes) and a part-time job keep her busy in the real world, but whenever she gets a moment's peace she loves to write romance novels in an array of genres, including regency, medieval and time travel.

www.tamaragill.com
tamaragillauthor@gmail.com

Manufactured by Amazon.ca
Bolton, ON